THE SEA DEVIL

PIRATES OF BRITANNIA: LORDS OF THE SEA

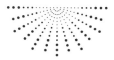

ELIZA KNIGHT

KNIGHT
MEDIA

Thornley "Thor" MacLeod, captain of *The Sea Devil* and prominent member of the Devils of the Deep is out for one thing and one thing only—revenge against Santiago Fernandez, leader of *Los Demonios de Mar*. Tormented by the demons of his past, he knows the only relief to his pain will be spilling the blood of his enemy. When he learns that Santiago seeks to find a child he abandoned nearly two decades before, Thor is determined to find the precious treasure first. Which means, Thor may have to sacrifice his honor in order to exact the perfect vengeance.

Orphaned at a young age, Alesia Baird has grown up along the harsh coasts of Scotland, bearing witness to many a nightmare. With the hangman's noose dangling ever closer to her neck, she has to find a way to escape the only life she's ever known. When she overhears a pirate mention he seeks the child of Santiago Fernandez, Alesia takes the leap, knowing this could be her only way out.

Alesia must keep up the ruse long enough to escape with her life, and perhaps a sack full of jewels. But when it comes time to jump ship, she finds her destiny may have led her in a different path. Will the hardened Highlander allow a lass into his heart—or is she destined to be alone forever?

MORE BOOKS BY ELIZA KNIGHT

PRINCE CHARLIE'S ANGELS

The Rebel Wears Plaid
Truly Madly Plaid
You've Got Plaid

THE SUTHERLAND LEGACY

The Highlander's Gift
The Highlander's Quest
The Highlander's Stolen Bride
The Highlander's Hellion
The Highlander's Secret Vow
The Highlander's Enchantment

THE STOLEN BRIDE SERIES

The Highlander's Temptation
The Highlander's Reward
The Highlander's Conquest
The Highlander's Lady
The Highlander's Warrior Bride
The Highlander's Triumph
The Highlander's Sin
Wild Highland Mistletoe (a Stolen Bride winter novella)
The Highlander's Charm (a Stolen Bride novella)
A Kilted Christmas Wish – a contemporary Holiday spin-off
The Highlander's Surrender
The Highlander's Dare

THE CONQUERED BRIDE SERIES

Conquered by the Highlander
Seduced by the Laird
Taken by the Highlander (a Conquered bride novella)
Claimed by the Warrior
Stolen by the Laird
Protected by the Laird (a Conquered bride novella)
Guarded by the Warrior

THE MACDOUGALL LEGACY SERIES

Laird of Shadows
Laird of Twilight
Laird of Darkness

PIRATES OF BRITANNIA: DEVILS OF THE DEEP

Savage of the Sea
The Sea Devil
A Pirate's Bounty

THE THISTLES AND ROSES SERIES

Promise of a Knight
Eternally Bound
Breath from the Sea

THE HIGHLAND BOUND SERIES (EROTIC TIME-TRAVEL)

Behind the Plaid
Bared to the Laird
Dark Side of the Laird
Highlander's Touch
Highlander Undone
Highlander Unraveled

WICKED WOMEN

Her Desperate Gamble
Seducing the Sheriff
Kiss Me, Cowboy

HISTORICAL FICTION

Coming soon!

The Little Mayfair Bookshop

TALES FROM THE TUDOR COURT

My Lady Viper
Prisoner of the Queen

ANCIENT HISTORICAL FICTION

A Day of Fire: a novel of Pompeii
A Year of Ravens: a novel of Boudica's Rebellion

FRENCH REVOLUTION

Ribbons of Scarlet: a novel of the French Revolution

LEGEND OF THE PIRATES OF
BRITANNIA

IN THE YEAR OF OUR LORD 854, a wee lad by the name of Arthur MacAlpin set out on an adventure that would turn the tides of his fortune, for what could be more exciting than being feared and showered with gold?

Arthur wanted to be king. A sovereign as great as King Arthur, who came hundreds of years before him. The legendary knight who was able to pull a magical sword from stone, met ladies in lakes and vanquished evil with a vast following who worshipped him. But while *that* King Arthur brought to mind dreamlike images of a round table surrounded by chivalrous knights and the ladies they romanced, MacAlpin wanted to cause night terrors from every babe, woman and man.

Aye, MacAlpin, king of the pirates of Britannia would be a name most feared. A name that crossed children's lips when the candles were blown out at night. When a shadow passed over a wall, was it the pirate king? When a ship sailed into port in the dark hours of night, was it him?

As the fourth son of the conquering Pictish King Cináed, Arthur wanted to prove himself to his father. He wanted to make his father proud, and show him that he, too, could be a conqueror. King Cináed was praised widely for having run off the Vikings, for saving his people, for amassing a vast and strong army. No one would dare encroach on his conquered lands when they would have to face the end of his blade.

Arthur wanted that, too. He wanted to be feared. Awed. To hold his sword up and have devils come flying from the tip.

So, it was on a fateful summer night in 854, that at the age of ten and nine, Arthur amassed a crew of young and roguish Picts and stealthily commandeered one of his father's ships. They blackened the sails to hide them from those on watch and began an adventure that would last a lifetime and beyond.

The lads trolled the seas, boarding ships and sacking small coastal villages. In fact, they even sailed so far north as to raid a Viking village in the name of his father. By the time they returned to Oban, and the seat of King Cináed, all of Scotland was raging about Arthur's atrocities. Confused, he tried to explain, but his father would not listen and would not allow him back into the castle.

King Cináed banished his youngest son from the land, condemned his acts as evil and told him he never wanted to see him again.

Enraged and experiencing an underlying layer of mortification, Arthur took to the seas, gathering men as he went, and building a family he could trust would not shun him. They ravaged the sea as well as the land—using his clan's name as a lasting insult to his father for turning him out.

The legendary Pirate King was rumored to be merciless, the type of vengeful pirate who would drown a babe in his mother's own milk if she didn't give him the pearls at her neck. They were mostly steeped in falsehoods meant to intimidate. In fact, there may have been a wee boy or two he saved from an untimely fate. Whenever they came across a lad or lass in need, as Arthur himself had once been, they took them into the fold.

One ship became two. And then three, four, five, until a score of ships with blackened sails roamed the seas.

These were *his* warriors. A legion of men who adored him, respected him, followed him, and together they wreaked havoc on the blood ties that had sent him away. And generation upon generation, country upon country, they spread far and wide, until people feared them from horizon to horizon. Every pirate king to follow was named MacAlpin, so his father's banishment would never be forgotten.

They were lords of the sea, a daring brotherhood where honor among thieves reigned supreme and crushing their enemies was a thrilling pastime.

These are the pirates of Britannia, and here are their stories…

CHAPTER ONE

Edinburgh, Scotland
1445

Though he wasn't drunk, he was perfectly willing to let every other buffoon in the tavern believe it were so.

Thor, Captain of *The Sea Devil*, and longtime second-in-command to the Prince of the Devils of the Deep brethren, often played this game.

The thing was, when a dunce believed Thor to be deep in his cups, he often joined him, and when a man was liquored up, his tongue became loose as a tavern wench in need of coin. And that was how Thor often found out about treasure that needed saving, or heads that needed bashing. Verily, the usual squealers were the swain with enough ale or whisky in their bellies to widen their jaws and wag their tongues.

As it happened, right now, a very intriguing conversation was taking place a few tables away. Talk of pirates and gold—two things that were liable to interest anyone in the tavern, not just Thor.

Letting out a belch loud enough to shake the rafters, Thor tapped his mug on the table rather obnoxiously and shouted, "Another! And shome for my"—he waved his hands in the air and pretended to tip back on his chair, balancing mid-air before righting himself with a snort of fake laughter—"all my friendsh."

The men in the tavern let out a loud round of whoops and hollers, clicking their mugs as the wenches scurried to fill them with ale up to the rims and collect the coin from Thor before he changed his mind. On the far side of the tavern, men broke out in song, boot heels tapping against the sagging wood of the floor. The torches danced precariously in place where they hung on the walls. One of the drunkards picked up a set of bagpipes and began to play a rather dismal and shameful rendition of a Highland ballad.

Well, that wouldn't do. Thor charged across the tavern, making certain to bounce against a few backs, spilling his ale and appearing unstable as he made his way there.

"That ish not how 'tish done," he slurred. "Let me show ye."

"Ye?" the buffoon laughed. "Another round says ye fall on your arse when ye blow."

Thor grinned. "And if I do, I'll shtill keep on playing." Lord, help him, but he hoped the men discussing gold and pirates fell for his act.

Thor grabbed the pipes, settled them against his shoulder, left hand holding the chanter, right hand on the bag. He blew into them, and the squealing sound that issued was enough to have the men falling over laughing. But once he had a handle on the pipes, he played a haunting melody he'd penned on the high seas. The men of the tavern couldn't hear the words he'd created to go with the song. No one would ever hear them twice, for he changed them in his mind each time.

When he finished the song, he dutifully fell to his arse with a laugh, tossing the pipes back to their owner.

"Impressive, ye drunk bastard," said the man as he caught the pipes.

"No matter how drunk, a man always knows how to play his pipes," Thor said, bringing out a round of laughter from the men. "Drinks on my friend here!"

As the wenches moved to refill the cups, Thor climbed to his feet, glancing out the side of his eye toward the men he'd been spying on earlier. They were still there, still talking in hushed tones. They'd stopped while he played, mesmerized as everyone else was by Thor's sea song.

He wagered the time to be nearing midnight, and most of the rapscallions in the place had been splashing ale and whisky down their throats for the better part of several hours.

Thor staggered around the tavern, pretending to drink his empty cup of ale and slapping random men on their backs. To keep his ruse going, he shared a juicy tidbit about a wench he'd bedded the day before—a total lie—but it drew him closer to the table huddled in the corner, which was what he wanted. Thor didn't bed women simply to brag about it, but for some reason, bawdy jests and innuendo always seemed to open men up, and so he'd use that to his full advantage.

"Aye, he'll be paying a hefty sum in gold," said the man farthest at the table from Thor.

Thor listened to their conversation as he continued being rowdy with the men at the table beside them.

"How much?" one whispered.

"I heard tell it was an entire chest of gold. A king's ransom."

"For a wee bairn?"

A wee bairn... What in the bloody hell kind of treasure

was that? What pirate wanted to deal with a child? Thor could barely stand the adolescent lad he'd helped his pirate prince Shaw "Savage" MacLeod rescue just a few months ago. The lad followed Thor around like a puppy. Well, until Thor snarled.

"Well, 'tis not a bairn no more," they continued, and Thor let out a loud belch to his newfound friends, which inspired a round of who could belch the loudest.

"How old?" The men looked about, none of them seeing Thor's side-eyed glance.

"He said twenty or so."

What in Hades were they talking about? Thor resisted the urge to knock their heads together and insist they spit the information out faster.

"Lad or lass?"

"He's not sure."

"Ye mean to tell me, Santiago Fernandez put out the word that he'd pay a king's ransom for a bastard he got on a Scots lass two decades ago, but he's not certain if it be a lad or lass?"

Whoa now... Thor almost choked on his empty mug. Santiago... Had he heard that correctly?

"Aye. A Scots whore. Santiago's got a bastard running around if 'tis still alive."

An icy chill rushed through his veins at the mention of Santiago Fernandez.

Thor growled, letting out a low curse, which startled his new friends.

"I need more ale!" he shouted, pretending that was the reason for his outburst.

A wench was by his side in less than a second, filling his mug as she rubbed her ample bosom against the front of his shirt. He winked at her, made to reach for one of her breasts, but she playfully batted his hand away. The men at his table laughed, but Thor felt no humor. Rather, he was seething inside at what he was hearing.

Captain Santiago Fernandez was his mortal enemy. Hate didn't even begin to explain how Thor felt about him. He loathed the man. And for good reason. The first time Thor ever laid eyes on him was when the Spanish pirate stood over the body of Thor's mother, laughing. The bastard had killed her. Murdered her in cold blood and left her bloodied and battered body on display for everyone to see, including Thor when he was just a lad. Santiago was the reason Thor had become a pirate two decades before. Five years ago, he'd thought the day of reckoning was at hand, but the bastard leader of *Los Demonios de Mar* had outmaneuvered him, then captured and tortured him. But that didn't mean Thor was going to give up. Their parting words all those years ago had been Thor's vow to see Santiago dead.

"Where'd ye hear it?" one of the scheming swain asked.

"From one of his crew. They were bragging about how they'd be the first to find Santiago's offspring." He leaned closer. "So I shanked him."

A plan started to formulate in Thor's mind. A crazy idea.

If these men were willing to kill for the information, the promise of a king's ransom had to be accurate. Why else would they gut each other for it? Aye, they were all a bunch of scoundrels, but they didn't kill just to kill, not without cause.

How many years had Thor waited to exact his revenge on the bastard? Was it just coincidence that the perfect opportunity had just presented itself? Or was it fate?

Thor didn't believe in fate. Nor did he believe in coincidences. But he did believe in luck, and today was turning out to be his lucky day.

A slow grin covered his face, and he pretended to throw back another swig from his empty cup—the contents of which he'd surreptitiously poured into each man's cup as he clinked mugs with them. He tossed the barkeep a sack full of coins, which he always did to maintain the secrecy of his identity, then waited outside the tavern until the three men who'd been whispering about Santiago's bairn stepped through the door.

Thor wasn't a small man. Even as child of ten, he'd been taller than most men in his mother's clan. She was a MacLeod, and after his bastard Viking father left his mother to the care of her family, Thor had repudiated any connection to the whoreson—but he couldn't deny it when he glanced at his reflection. For a long time, he'd shaved the wheat-colored hair from his head, only recently growing it out because he realized how much more savage it made him appear. Being a pirate was all about appearances. The only physical trait he'd inherited from his mother was her blue eyes. Thank God for that, because it meant when he did peer at his likeness, he could still make eye contact with himself, for he saw her instead of his traitorous father.

He was well over six and a half feet tall, and weighed as much as an ox. Even still, he was quiet, and the three men didn't hear him approach. He bashed one on the head, knocking him out cold, then he grabbed the other two by the scruffs of their necks and jerked them into the alleyway behind the tavern.

One of the men pissed himself before passing out. The other stared at Thor as though he were God or the devil, it made no difference.

"Tell me where I can find the bairn?" Thor demanded.

The scab's eyes widened, knowing instantly to whom Thor referred.

"I...I dinna know."

"Then how were ye planning to find him?"

"Might be a her."

Thor tightened his grip on the back of the imbecile's neck and leaned in closer. He spoke slowly, pronouncing each word in a clipped tone. "What was your plan?"

"We were going to put the word out. Offer a small reward for information."

"And then take the larger reward."

"Aye."

Thor nodded. "Sounds like a solid plan. And what makes ye think that the child survived?"

"No telling." The man was shaking so hard he vibrated Thor's arm.

"Here's your new plan—go home and pretend ye never heard of the bairn, or risk me finding ye and tearing your arms off and shoving them up your arse."

"Aye, sir." He nodded emphatically. "Aye, never heard of whatever it is ye speak of."

Pressing his lips together in thought, Thor head-butted the scab and dropped him to the ground beside his friends.

Sounded like as good a plan as any.

Thor grunted and nodded to himself again. This was truly happening. Revenge for his mother, for himself, for every man, woman and child Santiago had ever harmed, was within reach. Retribution would be his. And he refused to think of the bairn as being one of those victims, though guilt did prick his gut for it was likely true.

He stepped over the sleeping shites and made his way down to the wharf. The sun would soon be rising, and he needed to make certain his crew was on board with this newest mission, and that the reward of a chest full of gold and the satisfaction of revenge was well received.

A slow grin filled his face. Aye, soon he'd have Santiago's child tossed in the dark cell of *The Sea Devil*. He'd arrange to meet with the Spanish captain and toss the body at the man's feet—for he absolutely could not let a child of Santiago live, not when the man wanted it badly enough to offer such a massive reward. Then, when knowing dawned on the bastard's face, Thor would sink his blade deep into Santiago's heart. Revenge complete. An eye for an eye. A loved one for a loved one.

Thor ignored the bitter taste his own thoughts left on his tongue. He was a pirate. This was what pirates did. They ravaged, maimed, stole, took lives. Part of the brethren code he'd vowed to keep was not taking a life unnecessarily. But there had to be someway to get around that.

As he marched toward his ship, anyone scurrying around the docks at this bleak hour leapt out of his way, not wanting to cause trouble with a man the size of a mountain. The rest of them stayed where they were, hidden in the shadows, waiting for someone more vulnerable to pass by. Bodies heaved. Moaned. They were all up to no good.

Thievery.

Assault.

Smuggling.

Debauchery.

Thor had seen it all. And honoring the code of the brethren, if he came across an innocent being abused, he always stepped in. While he thought on it, he watched a lass leap across several barrels as two wharf guards chased her, their swords clinking as they shouted at her about the promise of the hangman's noose. She was dressed in breeches, but there was no hiding the feminine curves she was blessed with. The moon lit off her creamy skin and the flash of her wicked smile. Added to that, her hair fell loose of its plait in wild black curls that surrounded her face like a shroud of devilry. Och, Thor liked her. A lot. Had he not been on a mission, and she not running—quite well, might he add—from the authorities, he might have asked her to join him aboard his ship for a dram.

Thor grinned, watching her impressive dodging. She thrust one long leg out to catch the top of a barrel with a dainty foot, making running from wharf guards look like an elegant dance. The lass was clearly used to being chased by the authorities—and with getting away. She taunted them with lewd remarks he'd never heard come from a lass's lips and made a rude hand gesture at them as she darted into a darkened alley.

That was a lass who could take care of herself. His kind of woman.

Chuckling, he sauntered off, thinking it might be fun to go after her and offer her that dram after all, but she'd likely take his offer of respect as him wanting something else, and he might end up with a knife in his gut. Or worse—his ballocks.

Better to mind his own business. And keep his precious parts.

The Sea Devil loomed before him, the Devils of the Deep flag safely hidden and the merchant's flag swaying in the evening breeze in its place. Every time he saw her, his heart swelled as it had the first moment he'd found out the ship was his. It was after he'd escaped from Santiago. Shaw had seen fit to give him the twenty-two-gun galley in an effort to turn his mind from revenge and back on the brethren. The responsibility of being the captain had been exactly what Thor needed to get his head back in the game. His men respected him. He respected himself. He had more to focus on than just the revenge he'd lived and breathed for the better part of two decades. But that didn't mean he'd forgotten. Nay, he'd been a wild animal in hiding. Hibernating that need for vengeance until the right time presented itself. As it just had.

Thor leapt the few feet to the rope ladder and climbed. They never left a plank out for any scoundrel to climb aboard. That was asking for trouble. Trouble they did not need. Or want. The ship deck was littered with swabs, half of them drinking and cavorting, and the other half dead asleep.

Thor picked up his bagpipes, licked his lips, blew into the pipe, setting the tone for the music and then gave it his all, playing the same ballad he had in the tavern and longing for the seas to embrace them once more. Those who'd been asleep awoke, and those who'd been carousing quieted. They listened to their captain play, and when Thor was done, they waited for what he had to say.

"A treasure awaits us." Thor met each of their gazes, nodding. "A bounty at this port that will lead us to a chest of gold doubloons."

"Spanish gold," someone muttered with obvious pleasure.

"What kind of bounty?" another asked.

Thor grinned, settling his pipes back in their case. "'Tis the bastard bairn of none other than Captain Santiago Fernandez."

There were a few sharply indrawn breaths, and the men grew silent, waiting for their captain to expand on his words. He searched the sea of faces for Edgard, his first mate and second-in-command. Edgard's face was guarded, but he did nod his support. The man had been with him for as long as *The Sea Devil* had been his, and Thor trusted him implicitly.

"I dinna know if 'tis a lass or lad, but I do know he or she would be twenty by now. We'll put out the word for a small reward, and once we've the bastard in hand, we'll set sail for Scarba, and then arrange to meet Santiago to claim the gold."

"Ye're not going to give him the child." Edgard made the statement rather than asking, having picked up on Thor's choice of words.

"Nay. I'm going to kill the wee bastard. Kill Santiago. And take all the gold on his ship."

The men cheered, all except Edgard, who he suspected

would remind him of the brethren code when his men wouldn't dare. Thor took the large mug of ale they passed him, swigged it hard and then tossed it in the air.

He set his mouth to the pipes again and played a victorious tune, his hard gaze on Edgard's all the while. Screw the code. Vengeance would be his. The taste of sweet retribution was already thick and delicious on his tongue.

CHAPTER TWO

*a*lesia Baird leapt with glee from one barrel to the next, the rough soles of her boots planting firmly to the slimy wooden surfaces before she made her next launch. *Left. Right. Left. Right.*

A merry smile covered her lips as she bounded away from the blackguards who chased her. Aye, they were authority figures, wharf guards employed by the King of Scotland, but that mattered not to her. Authority figures were as bad as the devil himself as far as she was concerned. The bastards were after a few things she wasn't willing to give—bribes, punishment or death.

Today, it would seem death was on the line as they shouted to her about the gibbet she'd soon be hanging from. Her unmanageable hair had come loose from its tight plait, falling in a cascade down her back. As she ran, pieces flew in her face, stinging her cheeks and poking her eyes. And then her cap took flight.

Drat! That was her good hat, too, and she didn't have time to chase after it as much as she wanted to. Not unless she wanted to feel their rough hands wrap around her arms and yank her to the dark cell they called a prison.

Thank goodness, she'd not sewn any coins into it since she tended to lose the darned things.

If only she'd had the sense to steal the gown from her latest victim in addition to the brooch, then she might not be in this current predicament. As much as she hated gowns, given it was a life or death situation, she'd have tugged on the silly garment in an instant. Then she'd be sashaying across the dock dressed up like a lady, pretending she had a right to be there. Well, as much as any lady would be at the docks in the dead of night—perhaps more a lady of the evening. Alas, the brooch had been bright and shiny, and the lady's scream piercing enough that Alesia had taken flight rather than take the time to rob the snotty bird of her garments.

"Bugger off, ye blimey bastards!" she shouted behind her, adopting the language of the men of the wharf she'd heard often exclaimed for as long as she could remember.

Alesia Baird was what most common folk would call a wharf rat. Highly offensive if anyone were to ask her, but they didn't. They didn't care if they hurt her. In fact, they seemed to gain a certain amount of pleasure from beating the downtrodden. Well, they, whoever they were, could all rot.

Born to a beautiful lady of the night, Alesia could barely remember her mother now, having lost her when she was a wee one of just five summers. But what she did remember was the softness of her mother's arms. The sweet sound of her voice singing Alesia to sleep at night when she'd had a mind not to be too deep in her cups, or too angry about life in general. The smell of bergamot and sage that her mother wore to cover up for the lack of bath, and the abundance of male customers.

Aye, her mother was a lady of the night, and when she passed on, many of her customers thought it would be a good idea to bring Alesia into the fold. But even at the tender age of five, she'd known better than to allow for their *tender* ministrations. Instead, for the last fifteen years, she'd been driving the authorities mad with her antics, and surviving all the same.

Stubborn, strong and with a mean right hook, Alesia was a survivor. Something she told herself every night. No matter how they sought to tear her down, she wasn't about to let them get inside her head or her body, not if she could help it. They might promise her the gibbet, but that was being kind, and she was certain from past experience that they wouldn't be kind too quickly.

A few times, she'd been caught, beaten and abused, but those instances had only proved to make her fiercer, more full of hate for the bastards who'd done it, and more interested in finding a way out of this wretched existence. Away from Edinburgh, the Leith wharf. When she was younger, she'd dreamed of dolphins swimming up to the quay, and she'd leap onto their backs and ride away into the sunset. Naïve nonsense. If anyone was going to save her, it was going to be herself.

"This is the last time ye'll be stealing, ye wench!"

She thumbed her nail off her teeth at the fool, a most offensive gesture, and then leapt from the barrels to dart down an alleyway. Except the wharf guards were not the only two pursuing her. Two drunkards from the tavern had taken note of her running and decided to block the way, in hopes the guards would tip them.

"Back off," she warned, coming to a halt but not ceasing her movements completely as she bent her knees and shifted her weight from side to side, prepared to dive into a fray should she need to. From her periphery, she looked to see if there were any other men hiding in the shadows waiting for their moment to strike.

They chuckled, leering grins on their drunk-slackened faces and in their drooping eyes. "What's in it for us?"

"Walking away without a black eye. And your ballocks intact."

That only made them laugh harder, which sent a rush of hot anger pummeling through her chest. They clearly did not know her identity, or her reputation.

Behind her, she heard the rushing footsteps of the authorities come to a halting stop.

"Nowhere to run now, Miss Baird," one said.

"Sod off, Angus." Despite the calm indifference in her tone, her pulse soared. Two in front and two in back. Not good odds by any standard of measure. She'd fought multiples before, been paid to do it for entertainment. A good fight paid for nearly a month's worth of room and board in a tavern's taproom, sometimes more, but four men against her, two of whom were spitting mad and wanted her to dance the hempen jib... Not good odds at all.

They really did have her cornered.

"Your thieving has caught the eye of more than just us," the guard said. "Too many of the rich have warned the magistrate that if ye're not caught, they'll be sending in their own to take care of the problem. And, well, we canna have them going to such extremes. 'Tis not good for our business, lass."

"Ye're getting the noose," the second guard loudly proclaimed. "Time's come."

Alesia's throat tightened, a large lump forming there. This was a day she'd long since seen coming. After all, she'd gotten away with her thieving for far too long. Fighting was one thing, thieving was another.

The noose would soon be tightening around her throat. And no one would care. The bastard daughter of a whore. She didn't even know who her father was, but her mother had often told her he was a warrior. A man who'd passed through the city in need of comfort and care after battle and had chosen her mother. They'd lain together, and the gift of Alesia had been left in her mother's womb. When no other man had been able to get a bairn on her, this man had. And so her mother had thanked the stars for Alesia every single day—or at least she had once upon a time. In the last years of her life, her mother had found it hard to be grateful for a hungry child, a rotten one at that.

And now here that miracle-burden child was, cornered by a bunch of lying, thieving men with too much power to wield, and her life on the line.

She eyed her surroundings. The alley was narrow, the incline steep where the drunkards waited. Clothes out on lines above her head. Windows and doors shut tightly against her and anyone else. The ground was slick with filth, and there really wasn't anywhere to run but toward her assailants at the back or those at her front.

The drunkards would probably be a safer bet. Their reflexes were dulled by drink.

Faking a lunge toward the guards, she whirled on her feet, anticipating the lack of traction on the slippery stone walk. Using the momentum, she propelled herself toward the two drunkards, wrenching a dagger from her boot and jabbing at their bellies as they approached. One leapt to the left, away from her blade, which caught just a fraction of his shirt, nicking a rib. His own leap to avoid her caused him to skid out of control and topple to the ground, banging his head hard. The second drunkard watched his friend go down and must have thought better of confronting Alesia, as evidenced by his expression, but she wasn't going to give him that choice. Not when he'd been so unkind a moment before.

She jabbed her dagger toward him, and he took a fatal step and slid down the center of the slimy alleyway hill toward the two rushing guards. He fell into them, sending all three of them flying onto their arses. While she would normally like to stay and taunt them with her laughter, self-preservation bade her to run.

Alesia darted through the alleyways, her thighs burning at the uphill climb. She kept an eye out behind her to make sure she wasn't being followed. She could hear the two guards running around, asking if anyone had seen her, but no one would rat her out. Aye, they might all be a bunch of black-guards, and she a wharf rat, but they loved her all the same. Alesia never robbed from her fellow wharf dwellers, only from the rich nobles, and because of that, she was well respected among the commoners of Edinburgh.

The chase continued on for another two hours before the two guards gave up and went to bed. And thank goodness they did, because by then, Alesia's feet were killing her, her legs were so sore she might collapse, and her eyes were having trouble staying open.

She ended up curling up inside an empty crate she found at the end of a pier, and pulling the lid over her for protection should they come calling again while she slept. With her dagger clutched in her hands, she listened, prepared to launch an attack on anyone who dared open up the lid to her hiding place. When all seemed remotely quiet, she allowed her eyes to close and to drift into sleep.

An uncertain amount of time later, Alesia bolted awake at the sound of voices and a dim light coming through the cracks of the crate.

"Put the word out." The owner of the demand had a deep, resonating voice that sent a chill racing up her spine. "I want to have information on Santiago's bastard by nightfall so we can be on our way."

Bairn? At first she was certain they spoke of her, that it was a guard looking for her, although she didn't recognize the voice. But talk of a bairn meant they were looking for someone else.

"And the reward, Cap'n?"

She peeked through the cracks, trying to remain quiet and to catch a glimpse of those who spoke. But all she caught sight of were two pairs of leather boots—one average looking, and one pair that looked like they belonged to a giant with thick, muscled calves with knees at least six to eight inches above his companion. She could see the hems of their plaids, but the small crack in the crate didn't allow her to see any further.

"Enough silver to make their eyes cross." This was said by that deep, resonating voice again, which she decided belonged to the giant.

"Aye, Cap'n."

The giant sauntered away, back up toward the pier where several ships were docked, while the smaller man darted toward town.

When she could no longer make out their footsteps, nor anyone else's, Alesia crept from the crate, searched for anything to cover her hair, and settled on a ripped burlap sack as a shawl and hood. She followed the one headed toward town, observing as he stopped a man on the street.

"Name Santiago mean anything to ye?"

The man shook his head. "Should it?"

"Aye, he's a feared Spanish pirate."

The fellow's eyes widened with mockery. "Och, why didna ye say? We've a lot of those around here," the man said sarcastically.

Alesia stifled a gasp and then a laugh as the average-sized man from the dock socked the lad right in the face and grumbled, "Smartarse."

He changed up his speech a little bit with the next person he approached. "I'm looking for a bastard."

The newcomer chuckled. "Edinburgh's full of bastards. Good luck."

This truly was most intriguing. And entertaining. Alesia ducked behind a moving cart when a guard passed by. The merchant winked at her and then nodded when the guard was out of sight. She hurried to catch up with the mysterious man.

"I'm looking for the bastard of Santiago," he was saying to one of the tavern wenches.

"Canna say I've heard of him."

"Could be a lass."

"A lass, ye say? Plenty of those, too."

A bastard lass… Alesia's mind started to whirl with this new information. An idea was brewing, but not yet fully formed. She couldn't put her finger on exactly what it was, but she knew it would come to her.

"Ask your friends," continued the man from the wharf. "Cap'n Thor is looking. Silver for the one who finds him or her."

"Cap'n Thor, ye say?"

"Aye."

"I'll be certain to keep any eye out. What was the name of the sire?"

"Santiago Fernandez. Got a bastard in a woman about twenty years ago. Left her with nothing."

"Wouldn't be the first blackguard to do such a thing."

Certainly wouldn't, thought Alesia bitterly. Wasn't that her own past?

"Aye."

"Gonna be hard to find the right one. Ye'll be finding a lot of them sayin' they are him."

"Or her."

"Aye."

Captain Thor, a name that sent shivers up and down most

19

anyone's spine—fear for men and desire for women—was looking for a bastard born twenty years before, lass or lad. Had the giant been he? A shiver made her clutch the burlap sack tighter.

As far as Alesia knew, she was twenty years old. And if he didn't know if the one he sought was a woman or man, he might not know of any other defining features to look for.

With her life on the line, what did she have to lose by posing as the bastard Thor sought? And all that coin—it could be hers if she turned herself over to him.

With a purse full of silver, she could get away from Edinburgh. Start a new life. One that didn't involve stealing and running, or taking a beating because it was easier than facing death.

A warmth surged in her chest, one she didn't want to recognize as hope. Hope wasn't for people like her. She'd never had hope. Didn't deserve it. She was a thief. A wharf rat. Her mother had been a whore. She didn't even know who her father was—not that it mattered, since he'd left her mother without a second thought.

Perhaps he'd been a warrior, or perhaps he'd been a drunkard spewing lies her mother wanted to believe for the sake of the bairn growing in her belly.

No matter, Alesia had always only ever been able to count on herself. And if she wanted to see her fortunes change, she'd have to be the one to change them. Today, luck was on her side, even though she normally didn't believe in luck. Games of chance weren't her style. When a homeless wharf rat counted on the coin they could steal or the work they could barter for food and lodging, they didn't risk losing it to chance.

Following the pirate sailor as he made his way toward the taverns, she listened to him speak to a few more men, certain now that she could make this work, and knowing she'd do best to get back to Captain Thor's ship before anyone else.

Alesia backtracked until she found the crate and the pier the captain had gone down. Looming large in front of her was *The Sea Devil*, creaking and swaying in the retreating tide.

Men worked the rigging and brought various supplies onboard, and she watched them come and go, observing who they spoke to when they boarded. The men were watched like a hawk by a sturdy-looking sailor on deck. Sneaking on board was going to be harder than she thought.

Alesia grinned. Oh, how she loved a challenge.

CHAPTER THREE

A little wet and slightly nervous, but also proud of herself, Alesia sat on a cushioned chair in what she hoped was the captain's quarters and put her bare feet up on the wide, pristine wooden desk. As soon as she'd shimmied through the porthole, she'd discarded the wet boots in favor of not having wrinkled toes for days.

She wiggled her toes and rubbed her hands over her wet arms in hopes of getting warm, but the chill of the water had sunk into her bones, and the cabin did not afford much warmth. Also, Alesia was fairly certain the chill had more to do with waiting for the massive captain to find her. Because once he did, there was no going back on what could be a fool's plan. To distract herself, she stared about the stark wooden room.

The cabin was small, but better accommodations than any of the other men on the ship would have. The lowly swabs would all sleep on deck or in the hull in hammocks. But here, the captain had his own bed, which was tightly made with pristine starched sheets and a thick plaid blanket pressed down atop it. From the look of it, she wondered if the captain ever slept here. There were no discernible items set out to distinguish this room from any other captain's. No knickknacks set out or paintings on the wall. Not even a spare pair of boots tossed haphazardly in the corner. If she were to hazard a guess, Alesia would say that the man who inhabited these quarters did not want to put down roots. One runner could always recognize another. Or at least she liked to assume as much.

Across the room was a table nailed to the floorboards and four sturdy wooden chairs with nicks upon the arms as though someone had put a mark in the wood for every meal they'd eaten.

There was a chest at the foot of the bed that looked mighty interesting. She'd tested the dummy lock on the front and realized it was a fake. Finding the true lock and what was inside was her next course of action—after she convinced the giant she was *who* he was looking for. She couldn't risk being found by him and tossed off the ship before she'd even begun her quest.

Leaning forward, she opened up the drawers of the desk, finding the most mundane contents inside. A few scraps of parchment. Inkwell and feather pen. Not even a seal to reveal who the desk belonged to. Another drawer had a half-empty bottle of whisky, and the third drawer was locked. She considered picking that lock, too, for there was no other reason to keep someone out of the drawer unless there was something of value inside. This was a pirate's ship after all.

Alesia imagined handfuls of coin and jewels. Precious pieces she could pawn and live well for the rest of her life in comfort. Fed. Warm. Clothed. Safe.

Footsteps sounded outside the door and then the handle moved. Alesia sucked in her breath, suddenly feeling nerves that hadn't been present a moment before. Frozen, she stared at the slowly moving iron and then in agony as the door pushed open.

Captain Thor filled the entrance. The glimpse she'd had of his massive boots, thick calves and strong knees did little justice to the sheer size of him now. Picking her chin up off the floor, Alesia allowed herself to stare at him. And he let her, staring back as she followed a path from the top of his golden head to the tips of his long leather boots.

The man standing before her was easily a god. Had to be. He ducked through the door, and his startling blue eyes locked on her as though he wasn't the least bit surprised to see her sitting barefoot at his desk. Keeping his gaze on her, he shut the door, leaned back against it and crossed his thickly corded arms over his broad chest. The black shirt pulled taut against his arms and shoulders but billowed open at the neck. Shirt ties tipped with pagan-looking beads at their ends hung loose down his middle. The shirt was tucked into a plaid of dark reds, golds and a green so deep it was almost black, settled around his narrow hips, with a swath of it tossed and pinned over one shoulder. Just below the hem of his plaid were knees and impossibly long legs that looked carved from stone.

Never had she seen a man as huge as this one before. Massive. Gigantic. It made her question whether gods could walk on earth, and if a man could be so beautiful as to be breathtaking.

His wide, full lips were surrounded by a soft, short beard the same golden color as his hair, and though he didn't smile at her, there seemed to be humor dancing in his eyes all the same.

The moments ticked by without him saying a word. Instead, he just watched her. His ice-blue gaze raked over her, assessing, making her wish she had taken the time to at least bathe before boarding, though she supposed it wouldn't matter after her dip in the quay. Her bare toes were only a few feet from him, still propped up on his desk, and she was suddenly aware for the first time that her feet were not delicate like other women. They were hard and rough, just like the rest of her. Heat filled her cheeks, but she forced herself to remain strong. Indifferent. Callous as a pirate might be. When his gaze landed on her feet, she began to tremble but somehow managed to keep her quaking from becoming visible.

Alesia expected some sort of reaction from him for disrespecting his private space, but he didn't appear to be bothered in the least—or else he was incredibly good at hiding his emotions. The latter is what she suspected to be true. For she was also hiding how he affected her.

Finally, unable to stand it any longer, Alesia broke the silence. "I heard ye were looking for me, Viking."

His lips quirked into something similar to a grin. "And who might ye be?"

"Alesia Baird."

"Last time I checked, I wasna looking for a wee sprite."

Alesia raised a brow at his insult. "A wee sprite ye say?"

"Aye." He hadn't moved from where he stood, and the mirth in his gaze remained, as did that soft hint of a smile beneath his beard.

Unaware of why, but aware all the same, she found his confidence quite irritating. "I'll have ye know this *wee sprite* could take ye on any day of the week." She crossed her arms over her chest and worked to give him her very hardest glares.

The beast had the gall to laugh at that, not even concerned in the slightest by her bravado. "Is that so?"

Alesia grit her teeth, managing to push out an, "Aye."

The lopsided grin was unmistakable now, shining through the beard to irritate her all the more. "I'd like to see ye try."

Alesia was not one to ever beg off from a challenge. She'd not have made it this far on the wharf if she did. She had plenty of friends who'd succumbed to what they thought might be an easier life. Lifting her skirts for a scrap of bread and a cup of ale wasn't in Alesia's repertoire. But she was willing to raise her fists.

Slowly, she uncrossed her ankles and placed her bare feet on the cool floor. She rose, and droplets from her wet clothes fell to the wooden planks. Despite being soaked to the bone, she wasn't cold anymore. A strange heat had filled her upon seeing Captain Thor bracing the doorway, and then her irritation had warmed her all the more. Now, the rush of anticipation, of showing this fool what she was made of, thawed the remainder of her chill.

"Why ye're just a teeny thing." Captain Thor looked her up and down, eyes lingering on her bare toes. "Where are your shoes?"

"Ye're trying to distract me." She took another step closer to him, gauging just how much taller he was, what his girth was. If one were to enter a fight, all the better to know just what one was up against. "Dinna pretend ye care about my lack of shoes."

Mirth danced in his too-mesmerizing eyes. "Nay, dinna mistake my meaning, lass. I but wondered… at the smell."

Alesia's mouth dropped open. "What?" Did he just say what she thought he'd said?

"Ye heard me." A slow, wicked grin.

Oh, how she wanted to beat him for his insult. "Are ye suggesting my feet smell?"

"I'm nay suggesting it, love." He waved a hand in front of his face and rolled his eyes as though he might die.

Of all the... Molten-hot anger rushed through her. Alesia took that moment to strike. With her fists raised, she jabbed him right in the chin. Her knuckles cracked against his firm jaw, the hair on his face prickling her skin. *Bloody prig. That hurt.*

He didn't move.

But he did start to laugh, which only made Alesia rage all the more.

"Oh," she growled and jabbed him in the chin again with her other fist.

This time he slapped his knee, tears wetting his eyes. "Does this work for ye normally, lass? Or are ye jesting with me?"

Perhaps she was holding back. Anger sometimes did that. She wasn't concentrating enough. Focusing on her target, she took a deep breath in and out of her nose. He seemed to be waiting for her, almost giving her permission to punch him again. The pirate was built like an ox. And how could she possibly beat an ox? Clearly, his jawbone was made of steel.

A slow grin filled Alesia's face, mirroring that teasing mirth he'd been dishing out since they met. There was one place she knew she could hurt a man no matter his size and strength. But did she want to play dirty?

The way he taunted her now, waving her closer as he laughed, she decided that, aye, she *did* in fact want to play dirty. Without a thought otherwise, Alesia launched her third attack, faking a left hook toward his jaw again and putting the full force of her strength into a right-handed jab at his Highland pirate jewels. Her fist made connection with his vulnerable parts, and before she had time to dwell on the size and shape, she leapt back and out of his reach.

The man's face turned as scarlet as the red in his plaid, eyes bulging, the scar on his face turning white. She had to hand it to him, he didn't howl like the bastards she'd crushed before.

Captain Thor sputtered, "Och, lass, ye just punched me in the ballocks…"

Alesia didn't even blink at his use of vulgar language. "Do ye want another?"

"Mercy," he said through gritted teeth, watering eyes connecting with hers. "Ye did it on purpose?"

Alesia was unable to help her grin of triumph. "About my feet…" She wriggled her toes just beneath him.

"As sweet as the roses in any lady's garden," he choked out, the veins in his neck pulsing.

Now it was Alesia's turn to laugh. "Ye play the game well, Captain."

"And ye…" He coughed. "Ye play unfairly."

She shrugged, all serious now. If he thought she was going to capitulate on anything, he was mad. "Whoever said that life was fair?"

"Certainly no one ye've ever met." He rubbed his eyes with the heels of his hands and then ran a hand through his hair.

"And I'm guessing no one ye've encountered either."

The man straightened, reminding her just how enormous he was compared to her. Her gaze slid up his length, settling on the scar along his jaw.

"How'd ye get that scar?"

He raised a teasing brow. "What scar?"

Alesia rolled her eyes.

"Where'd ye learn to fight like that?" he asked.

"Fight? Ye call that a fight?" she scoffed, not wanting to reveal to this virtual stranger the rough life she led in Edinburgh. "I came here because ye're looking for me. Now, hand over the reward."

"Reward?"

"Aye, ye were offering a sack of silver. I'm here, and I'll collect on it."

Again, he crossed his arms over his massive chest, and she had the idea that if she tried to skirt around him to the door, all he'd have to do was reach out. His arms were long enough to span the room. "I'm afraid it doesna work that way, wee sprite."

She gritted her teeth. "Oh, ye great ogre?"

He chuckled. "Ye certainly have a way with words, lass. Allow me to explain. As I see it, I found ye. So I'll be keeping the treasure for myself."

Alesia shook her head, flexed her fists, sore knuckles popping. "If ye dinna give me what I'm owed, I'll be walking off this ship afore ye can rise up."

"Rise up?" He narrowed his eyes, scrutinizing her face and her balled fists. "Do ye plan to attempt castration again, lass?"

Alesia straightened her shoulders, trying to quell the anger and rising panic in her gut. Was he truly going to cheat her out of the silver? She had no choice but to get the coin and escape, else by sunrise she'd be in the hands of the wharf guards. She could only hide out from them for so long before they offered enough of a reward that even a saint would give her up.

Perhaps another tactic was in order. Cocking a shoulder coyly, she reached forward and tugged at the lace on his billowing black shirt, her fingers pinching a bead. "Certainly ye jest."

"I never jest." He appeared unmoved by her subtle flirtation, and in fact raised a brow, looking pointedly at her grip.

Alesia stepped closer to him, gazing up at him with practiced doe eyes. She'd seen seduction before in the alleyways and taverns. Had used it a time or two to scheme a mutton-head out of his dinner. "Would ye truly seek to abuse a lass?"

"Nay." There was a spark in his eyes that threw her off, as his arms snaked around her middle, hauling her taut to his body. Good God, he was so…hard. Everywhere. "But we both know I was not the one doing the seeking."

"What?" The question came out breathy as she tried to concentrate on something other than the way her breasts pressed to his solid chest, or that her nipples had tightened into points and how she kind of liked the way they sought the warmth of his body.

"Ye came here. Ye struck me—in the ballocks. Ye touched me just now."

He was right. But she didn't want him to be right. She placed her hands on his chest and tried to push away. "That doesna mean—"

"I'm a pirate, lass. What am I supposed to think when I come into my room and a lass has made herself at home, going so far as to take off her boots?"

She pushed against him more, and he did let go slightly, enough that she thought she might be able to draw a better breath, but it didn't appear that his hold was what kept her from breathing. Struggling to speak without choking, she said, "I came here because I heard ye were looking for the bastard of Santiago Fernandez."

"And ye claim to be that unfortunate offspring?"

She nodded solemnly. "I do."

"Prove it," he growled.

"How?" She wriggled against him. "Put me down first."

"Say something to me in Spanish."

He settled her in front of him, but not far enough away that she couldn't still feel the heat of his body sinking into hers. Thinking quickly on her feet, Alesia frowned up at him.

"My mother was Scots, and my father, the legendary Spanish pirate, abandoned me the moment he planted his seed, ye buffoon. Where would I have learned his language?"

"Point taken." He studied her face, eyes narrowed. "Ye do have the look of him. In a feminine sort of way. Save for that hair. Tempestuous hair."

Her mouth fell open at the insult. She moved to stomp on his foot but quickly found herself lifted off her feet, arms pinned to her sides by the steely strength of his own.

Fine, he wanted to play dirty. She'd already showed him once she knew how to take down a man. Alesia moved to kick him where she'd had the pleasure of socking him before, but Captain Thor clamped her legs between his thighs of steel.

"Uh-uh, princess," he mocked.

Though she hated to head-butt anyone for the headache it always gave her, that was her next move. Alesia was fairly certain at this point she wasn't going to be walking away with the silver, which meant she could at least walk away with her life—and figure out another way to escape the wharf.

Before she had the chance to make good on her decision to crack her head against his, she found herself flattened to the wood-planked floor, and his massive body on top of hers. Every hard plane pressed to the soft curves of her own. She sucked in a ragged breath, prepared to shout at him to leave off, but she found her throat too tight to speak.

"I'd have expected more from Santiago's daughter, wee sprite." His finger trailed over her cheek and along her jawline.

Alesia bared her teeth, trying to wriggle free but only managing to feel his body pressed harder to hers. "And I would have expected more from a pirate Captain."

"Touché." His grin was inviting. Unnerving. Disarming.

"Get off me," she growled, trying to keep her mind in the right place—the angry place. That was survival. To succumb to his disarmament was to lose.

His gaze shifted to her lips. "Not without a kiss."

Alesia snorted and shoved at his unmoving shoulders. "I'd not kiss ye if ye were the last man on earth."

"What if I were the second to last?" he teased.

She let out an exasperated groan. "Not then, either, ye ogre."

He clucked his tongue. "Shame."

"Why's that?"

"Because, lass, if sparring with ye is this fun, kissing would be even better."

She was momentarily stunned speechless by his words, but the laughter in his eyes spread to his lips and he started to chuckle.

"Oh, get off me, ye whoreson."

"Promise not to bite me when I do?"

"Ye'll have to pay me."

"We'll see." He climbed off her and backed toward the door.

Alesia glowered as she leapt to her feet, prepared if he should attack again.

"Calm down, kitten. I'm not going to flatten ye. Or try to kiss ye."

Kitten. Well, she liked that better than wee sprite. Alesia dusted at her wet breeches, noting that the front of his black shirt was darkened from her wet clothes. From his distance and stance, she was certain he didn't plan on tackling her again. And with that realization, something foreign snaked through her. What was this feeling? Disappointment?

Absurd. How could she be disappointed? She didn't want him on top of her again. Or did she?

She wasn't certain. But she knew she had no interest in

exploring it. Alesia didn't get close to people. When she did, they either died or cheated her. The only one she could count on was herself.

"Hope ye're prepared to meet your da. He's a real arse-hole." And with that, Captain Thor stormed from the cabin.

CHAPTER FOUR

Standing at the helm, Thor counted to six before the wee hellion emerged from his quarters and marched toward him across the massive deck of *The Sea Devil*.

Behind her, the docks had come to life with merchants, dockworkers, scum and all other beings that walked the slimy wharf. The people went about their day, completely unaware of the delight Thor was having in one of their own. And he wasn't the only one. 'Twould appear most of the crew was quite taken by the sight of her as well. They'd stopped their duties to stare slack jawed as she marched toward him.

He crossed his arms over his chest and eyed her. Saucy wench, and utterly irresistible. Aye, his ballocks had smarted, and the wee smack of her knuckles to his face had stung a bit, even still, he was mesmerized by her. He'd never met a lass like her. Hands on her hips, she marched toward him as his mother had done when he was a lad, ready to scold him. He wanted to doubt she was who she claimed, but she had the look of Santiago, however much more beautiful.

"I must say, I'm disappointed, ye wee sprite," he said,

trying for seriousness but certain his tone gave away his mirth. "I had thought it would only take ye three seconds to emerge, not six."

Alesia jabbed her finger toward him, prepared to say something quite unladylike, he was certain. But she must have thought better of it, because she clamped her mouth shut. She crossed her arms over her pert breasts, mirroring his stance, and then turned in a slow, barefooted circle to take in the ship and the crew as they worked the sails and prepared to debark. Her head fell back as she looked up at the masts, the loose sails, and the phony flag. Two ravens perched high on his crow's nest, squawking, and he thanked his lucky stars it wasn't three—a bad omen and a sign of death.

When she turned back to him, for a split second he saw the fear in her eyes before it was replaced with that over-the-top bravado she'd exhibited in his chamber. *Och*, he cursed under his breath. Why did he have to find her so mesmerizing when he ought to despise her, or better yet, feel indifference given what his plans were.

"Where are we going?" she asked softly.

Thor studied the wee firebrand. There was so much more to her than met the eye, and he found himself alarmingly intrigued. How was it possible his enemy had sired anything Thor took an interest in? When he'd thought Santiago's bastard was a male, he'd planned to toss the bugger in the jail cell of the hold below deck and be done with him until they found his miserable father. But when Alesia presented herself, his mind took a different turn altogether.

A woman. An enticing one at that. Even beneath the layer of a year's worth of dirt caked to her skin, he could tell she was bonny.

She was also a woman who'd had a rough go of it. A small part of his heart pricked with guilt. His code, the code of the brethren, was to care for the weak, and while she might theoretically fall into that category, Thor would bet the ballocks she'd tried to crush that the lass would be highly insulted to know he considered her anything other than a force to be reckoned with.

She didn't seem to want to be saved. At least that was what he was going to tell himself, because right now, an idea had begun to percolate in his mind, taking root as he watched her breasts rise and fall with each breath. They weren't large breasts, nor were they particularly small. Not his ordinary desire of plush, bouncing pillows that spilled all over him, hers would fit perfectly in his palms. His blood stirred as he watched and recalled how they'd felt pressed to his chest when he'd grabbed hold of her in his cabin. Soft, pert, with hardened nipples that had defied the bluster of her attitude.

"Get your mind out of the slop pot, sailor," she murmured.

Thor didn't bother jerking his gaze away from her breasts. He raised them slowly. "I'm no sailor, lass. I'm the captain of this ship, and ye'd do best to remember it."

She raised a challenging brow. "Best, would I?"

Och, she was trying his patience. He couldn't remember the last person who'd been able to get under his skin so well.

"Aye," he drawled. "Else ye'll end up in the bowels of this ship, locked behind bars with a bucket to piss in and a crust of bread to gnaw on, if ye're lucky."

She tossed her wild dark curls over her shoulder and gave him a smile filled with mockery. "Do ye treat all your prisoners to such pleasantries?"

Thor grunted and was rewarded with a roll of her fiery green eyes.

"Ye think I'd be scared of that?" Her arms fell to her sides, her shoulders sagging slightly. "I've been living on the streets of Edinburgh since I was a bairn, pirate. I've seen and been through worse."

It was on the tip of his tongue to ask just what that meant, but he held back, knowing that, one, she wouldn't answer and, two, he shouldn't care. *Stick to the plan*, he told himself. With the amount of gold doubloons Santiago was likely harboring in exchange for the lass, he could very soon find the Devils of the Deep a great treasure.

"So?" she urged.

"So what?"

"If your ship's dungeon is not my fate, what is it?"

Hell and damnation. He'd lost his train of thought again. "Ye'll see." Thor wasn't stupid. He wasn't going to tell her his plan until they were well out to sea and there was no way for her to escape. They may have only just gotten acquainted, but he was fairly certain she wasn't going to like his new plan. She might even prefer the dungeons. That only made his idea more of a challenge.

Another roll of her eyes. A huff of her breath. Breasts rising and falling. Och, but his mind wasn't going anywhere near a slop pot. Far from it. What he was thinking of was only pleasure.

"If ye keep doing that, ye might fall flat on your arse," he warned, but he didn't add, *with me on top of ye*.

"Doing what?" she snapped.

"Rolling those big green eyes."

"Green?" Her eyes widened, allowing the sun to shine brighter on them, giving off the effect of sparkling emeralds.

Thor gritted his teeth. Why did he have to think of her eyes in such poetic terms? They were eyes. Things to see with. "Aye," he grumbled moodily. "Havena ye ever seen your reflection?"

Alesia frowned, and for a split second, she gave off the impression of hugging herself tighter. "Not in anything

37

other than murky water. I thought my eyes were quite brown."

"Nay. Green, lass." That small spark of pity that had lodged itself in his gut presented itself once more.

"Huh." She bit her lower lip, looking toward her toes. "I suppose I should be embarrassed," she said quietly.

"Why? I wouldna be."

"Ye wouldna?" She peeked up at him, and it was plain to see she sought reassurance, so out of character from the lass he knew her to be.

"Nay." His voice had softened. They all had their vulnerabilities, and he wasn't going to judge her for the ones she harbored. Clearly, her appearance was one of them.

"Cap'n." Edgard, his first mate, bowed. "Message has been delivered."

"Thank ye, Edgard. Alert the crew 'tis time to push away." Soon Santiago would know that Thor had his offspring, and a meeting place would be established.

"Aye, Cap'n."

Thor kept his gaze on Alesia. Dark tendrils of hair fell wildly around her slim shoulders, covered only by a worn shirt. Her jawline was sharp, neck long, torso thin. It was obvious she'd missed more than a few meals, but despite that, she was still stronger than most females. Where their bodies might be soft, hers had been hardened, but she was soft in all the right places. Perhaps when she'd honed her skills at fighting, she'd gained the muscle he didn't normally feel upon a lass.

A slow grin covered his face.

"What are ye smiling at?" she asked.

He hadn't realized she'd turned to look at him over her shoulder as he'd perused the length of her. "Just thinking that it might be fun to have the men place wagers."

"On?" A skeptical gaze raked over him.

"Your fists."

An unladylike grunt escaped her. "I hope ye'd be placing wagers on me winning. I've not seen one of your men I canna beat."

Thor laughed loud enough that half the crew jerked their gazes toward him. He wasn't one for laughing. Rarely joked. But something about this lass had him thinking and reacting in ways he wouldn't normally. Quickly, he silenced himself.

"The swabs may look weak, lass, but trust me, the life of a sailor, and especially a pirate, is a hard one."

She sauntered back toward him, her bare toes so tiny beside his boots. "More so than the life of a wharf rat?"

"Ye will see."

"I suppose I will." She ran a finger over the helm, and he found himself utterly silent, because if anyone else, besides Edgard, dared to touch his captain's wheel, he'd hold a dagger to their throat. "How long until we meet Sant—my father?" A frown made her full lips thin and turn down.

"Ye dinna have to call him your father if ye dinna want."

"But isna that why I'm here?" She pushed her wild hair away from her face as the wind continued to whip it back against her cheeks.

"Simply because the man got a woman with child doesna make him a father, only a sire." He didn't know if she'd pick up on his insinuation that Santiago was an arse or not, but she nodded all the same.

"I should hate him." She pursed her lips, gave a dainty shrug of her shoulders, then moved to touch the rigging, and appeared to be working out the knots in her mind.

"For leaving your mother in a precarious way?"

Green eyes flicked toward him, all seriousness and calm. "For giving me life."

"Och," Thor scoffed. "The man didna give ye life. Only your mother and yourself can lay claim to that."

"He was a necessary part."

"A meal without meat is still a meal."

"Are ye calling Santiago a piece of meat?" A giggle escaped her, and for that brief moment, he glimpsed a spark of joy in her.

Thor grinned. "Maybe."

A smile spread on her lips, which gave him pause. Despite the grit that seemed to have found a permanent place on her skin, she was quite striking. It made what he was going to do more palatable, but at the same time, it made him think he should despise himself.

Thor shook off his misgivings. This was Santiago Fernandez's daughter. The spawn of his mortal enemy. The path to his revenge had seemed like a ray of hope yesterday, and now it was assured.

But it wouldn't be the dungeon for his prisoner. Nay, Thor was going to do what he did best—besides pirating. He was going to seduce her. Ruin her. And he was going to enjoy every damn minute of it, no matter how many times she tried to whack him in the ballocks. There was a fire and passion within her that he intended to wrestle out.

Rape wasn't his style—he'd never forced a woman. By the time he was done, she would be begging for him. And then, when they arrived at the designated meeting spot for him to present Santiago with what his seed had grown, he'd let the man know every single act of debauchery in great detail. Best of all, he might even plant a bastard of his own. Then, he would sink his blade into Santiago's heart with the knowledge that he'd taken everything for himself.

Before Thor could begin his wooing, however, the lass was in thorough need of a dunking. Thor wasn't a picky man, but he did draw the line at filthy. Without warning, he lifted her into the air and tossed her over his shoulder.

"What are ye doing?" she ground out among pummels to his back.

"Ye need a bath."

"Put me down!"

The men on the ship grinned as they hoisted the sails and the rowers below propelled the galley through the water and away from the port.

Thor couldn't help but grin to himself. She fought against him, kicking and shouting out obscenities that he bet half his men hadn't heard before. Hell, there were a couple he was unfamiliar with.

"'Haps I ought to wash out that charming mouth of yours, too."

"Ye'll do no such thing," she shouted, punching him hard in the middle of his back.

Rather than wince, shout, or toss her into the ocean, Thor smacked her bottom hard, gritting his teeth against the way her rounded rump bounced back against his hand. Heaven help him, but she was more than he could have hoped for in a bed partner, let alone one he intended to thoroughly ravage in every way.

Blood and bones, this was going to be good. Thor marched toward his quarters, hollering for a tub and hot water, and grinning all the more as she shouted for the men not to dare bring the items. Who the hell did she think she was? It was both funny and irritating. Of course, his men did not listen to her in the slightest.

Inside his cabin, he held her over his shoulder, taking her abuse until the tub, hot water, lye soap and rags were produced, then he tossed her into the tub, fully clothed.

Alesia sputtered, wiping the water from her face and glowering up at him. When she started to scramble from the tub, he *tsked* at her.

"Dinna even think about it. Ye smell worse than the

41

lowliest swabs on the ship. More so than the rowers below deck."

"So what? The better to repel the likes of ye." Och, but she was beautiful even when she snarled.

Thor chuckled. "Och, a little smell never repelled me from a bonny lass, especially since it isna permanent." He tossed her the lye soap and a rag. "Start scrubbing, or I will."

Alesia set her mouth in a grim line and glowered at him. She also did not lift the soap and rag. Didn't move an inch. So, she wanted to challenge him, aye? Didn't think he'd go through with his threats. Well, if she thought he wouldn't, she was only fooling herself.

Thor marched toward her, standing over the tub and staring down into her wet face, streaked with rivulets of water that revealed creamy skin beneath the grime. But even those few moments of waiting didn't produce results. With a subtle shake of his head, he rolled up his sleeves and snatched the soap and rag from the water.

"Ye're a stubborn sprite," he growled as he rubbed the soap onto the rag.

"Remove your clothes," he ordered, staring at the far wall.

"Nay."

His gaze snapped back to her. "Lass, I think ye know by now I'm not one to trifle with. Remove them, or I'll do it for ye."

"Why will ye not just leave me alone?" Tears gathered in her eyes, causing him to take a step back.

"I gave ye the chance to wash yourself. I'll give ye another." His tone had gone softer, kinder. He didn't want her to cry. Hell, how was he going to go through with his plan? When he least expected it, the vulnerable side of her reached out and bit him.

"Fine." She swiped angrily at her tears. "Turn your back."

Slowly, he shook his head. "I'll do no such thing, lass, else ye scrabble out and attempt to bludgeon me again."

"Avert your eyes," she ground out. "'Tis indecent."

Thor braced his hands on either side of the tub and stared into her eyes, daring her to argue with him again. "I dinna take orders from ye. This is my ship, and ye'll do what I bloody well tell ye." So much for a gentler touch. She had the ability to bring out a range of feelings he was not wholly familiar with.

"Ye dinna scare me," she said through bared teeth, her hair plastered to her forehead and rivulets of clear water making pink tracks through the muck caked on her skin. "I've spent my whole life running from men like ye. Thinking ye can touch me anyway ye want. To say whatever ye want. Take whatever ye desire. Well, I'm through."

His heart twinged. Hearing her say that spoke to him on a very different level. His moral code and oath to the brotherhood was to protect the weak and made him second-guess his decision to debauch her.

How could Santiago have left his daughter to suffer?

How could he take advantage of her when she was so plainly refusing to allow it?

She stood up, soaked to the bone, the dirty rags hewed to her body like a second skin.

Ballocks, was this just another trick? A way to make him pity her? To be kind to her?

For a moment, he had a flashing vision of his mother standing very much like this, but in the rain, facing down her attacker. Santiago Fernandez. But no matter how strong his mother was, no matter how much she represented the warrior Thor knew her to be, she'd still fallen when Santiago thrust his blade into her heart.

And even worse, he could see his father standing by and doing nothing to stop it. Worse still was knowing this father had been the one to invite Santiago into their home in the Highlands.

The bastard Spaniard had been willing to pay a hefty price for the fairy flag that hung in his clan's tower. And his father, a true Viking at heart, had never accepted the MacLeod clan as his family, his responsibility, his people.

Thor pushed away from the tub and the soaking wet woman. He was not his father. Yet the reflection of him in her eyes looked just as savage as the man who'd sired him.

"Finish your bath," he growled, turning his back on her.

CHAPTER FIVE

Standing in the tub with water dripping over her, Alesia shook from cold and indignation. She stared at the wide back of the pirate who'd just done the one thing he'd sworn not to. He'd turned around. Faced away from her. She could take advantage of this moment. Leap from the tub and show him just how violent she'd learned to be. Or she could sink back into the warmth of the water, take the gift he'd given her and savor it.

Bath was a foreign word to a lass like her. In fact, she couldn't remember a time when she'd had one. It was rare for her to be completely clean, and when she'd had the privilege to wash, it had always been from a basin or a loch. Never warm.

The warm water sluicing over her skin was like heaven, and she wished more than anything to strip off her clothes, sink into the warmth and let her mind wander away to better places. Imaginary places. A place where she was safe and warm and wanted for nothing. To escape.

But those were a fool's imaginings, and she wasn't a fool. She couldn't afford to be a fool. Couldn't afford to build

45

dreams and wishes, for then she'd feel the pain of disappointment all the keener.

So she stood there for several moments like an idiot, recalling to mind the subtle change in Captain Thor as he'd leaned over the tub as they sparred. The anguish that had flashed through his eyes. For a moment, her heart had reached for him, feeling a kindred spirit even if he wasn't willing to share, but she'd recognized that even he needed to hide. Thor had backed away from her, shaking his head and looking at her as though she'd developed a second pair of breasts—or maybe devil's horns, as she suspected he was a man who might enjoy a woman with extra parts to fondle. As he'd backed away, it had taken every ounce of willpower she possessed not to reach for him, to keep her hands at her sides, unmoving.

When he still didn't turn around, Alesia sank into the tub and reached for the rag and soap. She scrubbed her feet, her ankles and calves, her belly, lower back and neck. Oh, but the water was silky warm against her skin, and the scrap of cloth lathered in lye made her skin tingle as it turned from dingy to pink.

Reaching beneath her shirt, she washed beneath her arms, biting her lip to keep from audibly moaning at the pleasure of being in a clean warm bath. Alas, there was more to wash, but she couldn't reach those parts in particular with her breeches on. As quietly as she could, which proved not to be quiet at all given the sloshing water over the edges of the tub —and still he kept his back to her—she pulled off the worn garment from her lower half and washed parts that had never seen a bar of soap.

Done with that chore, she pulled her breeches back on and leaned her head back, allowing herself a moment of relaxation and feeling some of the tension ease from her shoulders.

"When I was a child, I used to sneak into the alley closes and stare through the windows into people's homes and watch as they went about their normal, boring routines. I was mesmerized and filled with jealousy." She reached behind her, twisting her hair into a long spiral and squeezing out the water, a faraway smile on her face. "I've never had a home. I've never had a bath. No one's ever washed my hair— until ye. Perhaps my mother did when I was a bairn, but I dinna recall."

She flicked her gaze toward him. He had yet to turn around. There was a tightness about his shoulders, one she understood. Being on edge. Listening. Waiting. Picking through the words and contemplating a reaction.

"Have ye always been a pirate?" Perhaps changing the subject would elicit something from him.

Just when she thought he wouldn't answer, he did. "Nay."

Alesia threaded her hands through her hair, tugging at the snarls. She'd never had the luxury of a brush either and used her hands. Even if she did have a brush, her hair was often as wild as a sea storm, and she was fairly certain untamable. "Where's your home?"

"This is my home." Thor crossed his arms over his chest, and she couldn't decide whether that was an improvement to the balled fists at his sides or not. "The brethren are my family."

"I see." She started to plait her hair, hoping that if she did it while it was wet, it would remain that way. "That's still lucky, ye know."

"Aye."

"I've been fighting to feed myself since I could walk. Even afore my mama died, she wasn't around much, and when she was, she was mostly deep in her cups."

"No child should have to suffer like that."

Alesia let out a bitter laugh. "There's hundreds of 'em like me." Finished with the plait, she asked, "Have ye a ribbon?"

"Aye." He backed up to the desk, tugged open a drawer and pulled out a strip of fabric. "Will this do?"

"Aye."

Still not looking at her, he backed up until she reached for the strip of blue and green plaid and tugged it from his fingers.

"My thanks."

"What did ye want with the coin?" he asked. "To save all those like yourself?"

She tucked her knees close to her chest and rested her chin there, shaking her head. "Nay. I'm not so gallant as that. I wanted it to save myself."

Thor grunted, and she waited for his judgment of her selfishness, but none came.

"I would have saved 'em if I could," Alesia mused, certain that she would as she had tried to help them when she was there. "But there's not much I can do with a noose around my neck." And that was the truth. Save them and die, or save herself. Perhaps a stronger person would have been more self-sacrificing. But she'd given up enough in her short life already.

"I've had a noose around my neck, and ye're right, lass, 'tis quite difficult to move at all."

She straightened slightly, looking over at him, studying that strong, broad back and imagining how anyone could have gotten close to tying one on him. "Truly? A noose?"

"Aye. Was on the gibbet, hanging there and waiting for the rope to cut off the air completely. Feet dangling. Hurt like hell. At least two score of men stood around me, swords drawn, ready to fight. I'd already put a dozen of their comrades in the grave as they tried to get me up there." He rubbed his neck. "Guess their rope wasna strong enough for me."

"Why didna they just stab ye instead of hanging?"

Thor chuckled. "I have no idea. Because they're idiots?"

"How did ye get away?"

His grin widened as he told the story, allowing her a moment to see that beyond the unforgiving countenance and vicious scar to his face, he was truly a handsome man.

"A couple of friends."

"Come now, tell me more, else I find myself in the same place and need to call on my friends."

"Shaw, the Prince of the Devils of the Deep, and our English brethren captain, Constantine. They staged a coup. Rolled a cart with a fully lit cannon right into the center of the bastards. Of course, the crowd went running save one stupid idiot who wanted to be a hero and make certain the prisoner was truly dead."

"Did he…get blown up?"

"To smithereens."

"And ye?"

"I hauled my legs up over the gibbet arm and out of the way. Sat atop it until Shaw and Con could cut me down. Then we were on our merry way."

"That must have been a sight to behold." She grinned down into the bubbly bath water, sad that it was starting to feel cold. In her head, she could picture the whole story and felt completely mesmerized by it. Had it even been in Edinburgh? She doubted it, for she was certain if it had been, she would have heard about it or gone to see it. A hanging was prime entertainment for those whose lives were poor or great.

"Aye, 'twas impressive. But nothing like the time Shaw and I had to save Kelley's arse."

When her teeth started to chatter, Thor tossed her a long

49

sheet of dry linen, though he didn't let go of the other end. This time, he was facing her. As she stood, Alesia caught his gaze raking over her body, no doubt taking in the two taut peaks of her nipples. But was it really catching him admiring her when he did so blatantly?

There was another subtle shift in him, a darkening about the eyes, and a shiver of…hunger passed through her. The shift in him this time wasn't anguish, as it had been when he'd leaned over her while she was in the tub. Nay, this was desire. A look she'd seen many times on men in taverns. What was concerning to her, however, were the sensations washing over her. She'd never felt them before… and they were alarmingly potent.

Thor took a step closer to her, and she found herself leaning just an inch closer herself, until she realized she might fall on her face, since she was still in the tub.

Alesia stepped from the iron bucket, took hold of the linen and tugged, but he wouldn't quite let go. Cold water dripped on the floor around her feet, and she curled her toes in. "I think we've been in this exact position before," she said, bringing to mind when he'd first discovered her in his cabin, and she'd dripped water onto the floor.

Saints, it was hard to avoid his gaze, and the more she stared into his eyes, the hotter her cheeks felt.

"Aye. But if ye'll be so considerate, I'll take a kiss over a punch to the ballocks." Strong fingers caressed over her cheek, and she fought the urge to lean into him.

Why did she feel like self-control was a struggle when she was around him? To behave or not to behave, seemed to be the constant question. Without thought, she wanted so very badly to be wicked.

No one had ever touched her the way he did. Softly. With a gentleness that had her hopes rising like the tide in a storm. *Dinna be a fool. He wants nothing from ye but what everyone else desires.* Tears threatened, and she forced them away, squaring her shoulders and willing her teeth to cease their chattering. She took a step back to put some distance between them.

Putting on a brave façade she didn't quite feel, Alesia snorted and answered his question perhaps a few beats too late. "What man wouldna prefer a kiss?" This time, when she tugged harder on the linen, he did let go, but he didn't back away as she wrapped it around herself. If anything, he drew closer.

"Ye should change clothes," he murmured, eyeing her wet garments from her shoulders to her ankles.

"Ah, aye, let me just get some from my satchel." She snapped her fingers, letting the sarcasm ooze from her tone as her lips turned down in derision. "Drat. I didna bring my satchel. Och, who am I jesting, I dinna have a satchel."

"Ye left all your possessions behind to board my ship?"

Alesia nodded, unable to voice the lie. The truth was, she had no possessions. All she had were the clothes on her back and, tucked deep in her boot, the corded leather bracelet her mother had worn until the day she died and a couple of shillings she had planned to use to pay for her next meal.

Thor frowned and raked his hands through his hair, finally pulling his gaze from hers as he looked around his cabin. "I think we can scrounge something up."

"I dinna need your charity, and I'd rather not be in your debt. Just give me the coin ye owe me, and I'll be on my way. To the shops," she hastily added.

He jerked his too-penetrating gaze back to her and winged a brow. "Ah, the reward."

"Aye. I'd be able to purchase a whole new wardrobe with that." And get the hell out of Edinburgh. The ship swayed gently, reminding her that they were no longer docked and on their way to wherever it was he'd said they were going.

"Is that what a wharf lass wants? A whole new wardrobe?"

She frowned, feeling his words cut deeper than they should. She was more than a simple wharf rat. She was more than just a lass wanting to be covered in silks and damask. So much more. But for the life of her, at that moment, she couldn't come up with anything clever to say, which only made her feel insignificant.

She jutted her jaw and clutching the linen tighter. "Nay. I'll keep what I have until ye hand over the coin."

"Ye're pretty certain I will."

The room was feeling smaller and smaller. "Aye."

"Whether I like it or not."

Was he jesting with her? Mocking her? "Something like that."

Thor grunted and backed toward the door with his hands up. "If ye say so, lass."

Her brow furrowed. "I do say."

"As ye wish."

What game was he playing now, being so compliant with her? She turned in a circle, watching as he headed for the door. But before he could open it, she asked, "What's in it for ye?"

That question seemed to stop him short. Sharp eyes assessed her, and she had the oddest feeling he was measuring if she was worthy of his answer.

"I but want to see a father reunited with his daughter."

"That's a load of shite."

"Ye've a vulgar tongue." But he grinned all the same. "Might want to curb it afore ye meet your sire."

Oh, she could have thrown something if she was willing to drop the linen. "I'll not be changing for *any* man."

Thor shrugged. "Suit yourself."

"I always have." And that was never going to change.

"And ye always have to have the last word, too, aye?"

She opened her mouth to answer with a most unladylike

retort but then though better of it as she realized he was only asking her a trick question. Trying to get her to say something. The stinking whoreson. Clamping her lips closed, she glowered at him.

Seeming entertained by that, Thor chuckled. "Stay put, lass. The men aboard a pirate ship aren't likely to be kind to a lass, let alone one who is sopping wet."

Alesia sniffed, looking down her nose at him. "Then ye'd best do your job as captain and warn them off."

He grinned, shook his head, muttered something under his breath and shut the door behind him, leaving her quite alone and cold.

Alesia had been alone her whole life, but for some unrecognizable reason, as soon as he left, she felt lonelier than she'd ever been before. The sensation was unsettling. Such feelings weren't her. She was iron hard. She was a survivor. She was a fighter. And yet, since boarding the ship and meeting Thor, she felt incredibly out of sorts. Perhaps it was a combination of escaping death and leaving behind everything she'd ever known? But she was certain there was more to it than that. For the first time in her life, she might have met someone who…what? He didn't care about her. That wasn't it. It was more like she'd met someone who didn't want to simply use her. Except, he had to be using her. The man was a pirate. He wasn't going to rescue a long-lost bastard out of the goodness of his heart. Truth in point, he'd not given her the silver yet.

And that meant she was in more danger than she realized, because her heart was telling her she was safe, but her mind knew the truth was the exact opposite.

As soon as they found a port, she was going to have to jump ship. That was all she'd wanted anyway. To leave Edinburgh and start a new life. If she had to, she'd steal something from somewhere aboard this ship that she could sell at port to get herself started.

Mind working tirelessly, she took the time to pick the lock of the chest at the base of the captain's bed, then dug through it until she found a pair of breeches she could fit her entire body into one leg of. That wouldn't do. Why the hell did he lock this thing anyway? There was absolutely nothing of value in it. A distraction for someone looking to rob him? Probably. She shivered as she searched for something— anything—to wear, and found the one thing she despised—a gown.

As a child, her mother had always dressed her like a lad, just in case, to keep her safe from any would-be ravagers of young lasses. When her mother passed, she'd kept it up. Passing herself off as a lad had helped her more than once. As time passed, she'd come to despise anything in a gown. The women in the alley closes of Edinburgh swatted their brooms at wharf rats, stuck up their noses at the orphans, or at least at her, and Alesia had always vowed she'd never be a gown-wearing, twiddle-brained, prig.

But just this once, because she had a plan and needed to make some coin, and the captain himself had given her the perfect way to do it, Alesia tugged on the rose-gold confection and spent at least an hour lacing herself up.

When she was finished, she worried slightly over whether or not her plan would work, but then she snorted. Men were men. And she knew how to manipulate a cocksure braggart.

In a world where she was constantly fighting an uphill battle and losing, this was one fight she was determined to win.

CHAPTER SIX

*T*hor stood at the helm of the ship deep in thought. It had been hours since he'd left his quarters, and his blood still ran hot from seeing Alesia doused in water, her garments clinging to her like a second skin. Breeches that left not a single inch of her legs to the imagination and a shirt molded to her perfect breasts and enticingly pointed nipples.

"I'm taking ye up on your offer," came a female voice from behind him.

He groaned, and refused to turn around. "Go back to the cabin." His demand was harsh, and he hoped it got his message across loud and clear. He didn't want her out here. Not with his men, and most definitely not with him.

Enough time passed that he hoped she'd walked away, but then she spoke, making his gut clench. "I said I'm taking ye up on your offer, Captain Thor."

"I made ye no offers." Why did his voice sound so strangled?

"Aye, ye did." Her soft footsteps sounded behind him.

"Will ye put on some bloody shoes?" he grumbled, but his

voice trailed off and his jaw slackened when he caught sight of her as she faced him across the helm.

The lass wore a too-tight gown the color of a summer sunset that strained impossibly against her pert breasts. The trollop who'd worn the gown before her had been amply endowed, though a good six or ten inches shorter. He dared not look down to see if her calves were exposed, because he was certain they would be, and already blood was pooling in his groin. Blood and bones, his cock seemed to be in a constant state of rock solidness since he'd come across the lass. First her in wet clothes, and now this ridiculous gown. She might as well parade around naked in front of him.

"Go back to the cabin," he repeated, this time through bared teeth in the hopes she'd take his threat seriously.

No such luck, for she crossed her arms over her chest. There was a subtle tearing sound, and she fisted her hands at her side and looked ready to stomp her feet. Just where the gown tore, he hadn't a clue.

"Are ye a coward, Captain?" Alesia tossed her head, the braid she'd fashioned out of her unruly hair whipping from over her shoulder to her back. The thing could be used as a weapon.

Thor despised when anyone called him a coward. "Ye're treading in deep water, lass. I suggest ye heed my warnings and return to the cabin afore I toss ye over my shoulder and lock ye there myself."

Ignoring him completely, she licked her lips as she drew in a quick breath "I challenge one of your men to a fight. For coin," she said loud enough for the crew to hear.

"Ballocks," he groaned under his breath.

"Not ballocks, ye maggot-brain." She rolled her eyes. "I'm serious. I need coin. As ye can see"—she spread her hands out and turned in a mind-numbing circle—"this gown simply will not do. And ye have refused to give me the coin that belongs to me for turning myself over to ye so that I might purchase a new one."

Keeping his frown, he stared her down. "And so ye wish to fight for coin."

"Aye," she said without hesitation.

With a sigh of resignation, Thor responded, "Then ye shall fight me. I'll not have any of these men laying hands on ye."

A wide, victorious smile filled her face. "Then let us go."

Thor glanced down at the gown, unable to help himself from teasing her. "Ye know the rules state a woman is to fight bare-chested," he said with a roguish wink.

Her mouth fell open, and she shook her head. "I've never been one to follow rules, ye blackguard."

"I didna suppose ye were," he said with a dejected exhale.

Alesia snorted. "Shall we?"

"Ye dinna want an audience?"

She cocked her head at him, narrowed her eyes. "An audience?"

"The men. A crowd to cheer on the victor."

She pursed her lips. "I see. I had thought ye wouldna want your men to witness your downfall."

That made him laugh. She was so damned sure of herself. "Ye're a cocky lass."

"Ha. I am self-assured. There's a difference."

"Won many a fight, eh?" He took off his coat and started to roll up his sleeves.

"As a matter of fact, I have." Her chin lifted another notch. "More than ye can likely count."

"Well"—he whistled for Edgard to take the helm—"let us see what ye're made of then."

Once his lieutenant had the helm, he came around toward her, rolling his neck from side to side as he cracked it. He tossed his hat to one of the swabs and then nodded to her gown. "It's a might tight. Will ye be able to move?"

"I'm not stripping down, if that is what ye're suggesting."

"Suit yourself." Lord, but she was a stubborn one. He'd never met a lass as obstinate as she was. In fact, somehow over the course of the day, he'd grown a soft spot for her. She reminded him a lot of himself.

Turning to the mast, he rang the bell for the men to come up on deck. The seagulls that had been perching on the mast bars took off, squalling their displeasure. Once the crew were assembled, Thor raised his hand for silence.

"The lass has issued a wager, and we've asked ye all to bear witness."

The men looked at each other and then between their captain and Alesia, confusion etched on their sea-worn faces. Thor tried not to grin. They didn't say a word, else risk getting a thrashing, but their curiosity was definitely piqued.

Thor cast a slanted glance toward Alesia, who stood tall, hands behind her back as though she were used to being announced at a fight. Who was this woman? She'd alluded to a rough life, mentioned she'd fought many times before. But just what was her game?

"Miss Baird has wagered a challenge of fisticuffs."

At this, two dozen pairs of eyes flew wide as the helm was round and mouths gaped like the caves along the coasts.

"What say ye? Shall I accept her challenge?" At this, he was inviting his men to voice their opinions.

Shouts of approval rang loud, and then Edgard, from the helm called out, "What will she win?"

This had all the men laughing their arses off, because none of them expected her to be the victor.

"She'll win this." Thor tugged a coin purse that jingled full of silver from his sporran. To give her the purse would be nothing for him. He had more than enough.

"And if ye win?" Edgard asked.

Thor's grin slowly widened as he turned to look her over. "Och, my prize will be much greater and entirely more satisfying than a little silver." Alesia's cheeks heated as his gaze raked over her body. "If I win, she'll not leave my bed for a week."

The men let out whoops and hollers that were likely to wake the dead at the bottom of the sea. For what pirate didn't like to hear about bed-sport when a beautiful lass was the one doing the playing?

"What say ye, Miss Baird? Are the terms amenable?" Thor caught her gaze, watched her struggle.

She looked ready to pop, her face red as flames and her eyes bulging with fury.

"Aye," she ground out. "On one condition."

"That is?"

"If I win, I want the coin, *and* to see ye walk the plank. Naked."

Thor threw his head back and laughed so hard tears came to his eyes. Following suit, his men also laughed. But their laughter didn't seem to make her waver one bit. "Will I be allowed back on the ship?"

Lips pursed she appeared deep in thought. "Aye."

"All right. I agree to your terms. Are ye ready?"

She nodded and reached for her sleeves, showing an immense strength as with one tug she ripped at the fabric, rending it up to her elbows. She repeated the move on the other side, baring her long, lithe arms, sculpted with oddly sensual muscle.

"Do ye not wish to at least don shoes?" he asked, staring at the wee pinkness of her toes.

"I hate shoes. Thought ye'd have caught on to that by now."

"I've noticed."

One of the swabs started to tap at a drum. A steady *bum, bum, bum*, as though one of them were being made to walk the plank already.

Thor had no plan to start the fight. That was all up to her. This was her idea, and he wasn't one to ever hit a woman. If she wanted to wager a fight with him, she was going to have to come at him. Thor's plan was to block her. To defend himself until she exhausted herself, and then he was going to sweep her up into his arms and carry her back to his quarters to gain his prize. All he had to do was make certain she didn't get a hit on his Scottish bag and pipes like she'd done earlier, because if she did, she'd gain a slight upper hand.

She stood before him, green eyes focused on his face, and Thor took in the way she presented herself. Steady. Determined. Strong. Over the course of his life, he'd faced off with any number of rough men. Well-trained men. Devils and the like. He'd even faced off with an infamous female pirate once, but even she had nothing on the strength he saw in Alesia's eyes. This was different somehow. She was different. Didn't have killing on the mind. She didn't have maiming as her end game. The lass wanted something. The coin. But why?

Why did that seem more important to her than meeting her sire? He knew she didn't want it to buy clothes as she kept saying. By the look of her when she'd first come on his ship, he would have said that fashion was not one of her pursuits. And considering she wore breeches and shirts, there were plenty of those on his ship she could have taken.

Perhaps she hated her sire as much as he hated his.

That was just another thing they had in common.

Thor grinned at her, unable to help himself. He didn't know why, but seeing her standing there like that made him happy. The lass wanted to punch his face in, and he was pleased about it.

Thor walked in a half circle with his hands at his sides, his men as silent as the grave. The lass watched him, her hands raised out in front of her. The stance looked trained, as though she'd been instructed. This was certainly not her first time fighting. Hell, he'd known that from the solid right hook she'd swung at him in his cabin.

But she'd need to bring more than a right hook to this fight.

Alesia watched him intently, her gaze never wavering. Eyes locked on his. He almost felt mesmerized by the green depths.

"I'm happy to dance, lass, but—"

Thwack.

As soon as he'd opened his mouth, she'd lunged forward, jabbing a fist into his gut.

The hit took more out of him than he wanted to admit. *Wow.* He'd not been prepared, his muscles not tightened. He might just have a bruise there on the morrow.

Tossing her a wide grin, he held up his arms, though he didn't form fists. He just meant to block her blows.

"I'll let ye have that one," he taunted.

"Is that so?" She winked.

Thor almost stumbled. Was the lass teasing him?

Allowing her to best him wasn't an option. And not because he couldn't bear to part with the coin. In fact, he could give a shite about the coin. What he wasn't willing to lose was the opportunity to bed her for a week.

A slow rumble on the ship started. At first it sounded like *despaired, despaired, despaired,* but then Thor realized they were saying *Miss Baird, Miss Baird, Miss Baird.* They were chanting the little hellion on. He didn't know whether to be appalled or to laugh at their bravado.

But he dared not look at them to offer a reaction and leave himself open to another shot.

Alesia started to shift back and forth on her feet, bouncing a little, and a grin seemed stuck on her face. She was enjoying this and the men's chants.

Thor beckoned her to begin, enough was enough. He couldn't take the next shot, but he wasn't going to wait here all night.

The wee hellion bounced to the right, jabbed out with her left hand, which he moved to block, leaving his right side open for the three quick hooks she lodged into his ribs.

Ballocks! That hurt.

Thor swatted her away, and she danced back and out of his reach. This really wasn't fair. He wasn't going to fight her back, and he couldn't let her win either. But it seemed that waiting her out was going to leave him bruised.

What did one do with a child throwing a tantrum? Or a young swab whose fury at the world had him swinging at any man who neared? Thor lifted them up. And he was going to steal her up too.

A second later, she darted at him again, attempting to fake to the right this time, but he didn't let her. He'd been waiting for it, so he reached out with one arm, snaked it around her waist, hoisted her off her feet and tucked her under his arm as he spun in a circle, her legs dangling in front of him, her head and arms behind him.

She let out a vulgar curse and punched and kicked, but without much momentum behind her assault, it felt like a few flies bouncing off his skin.

"Och, lass, what happened?" He laughed. "Not so cocky now are ye?"

Just then, a sharp pain seared through the back of his thigh. It felt remarkably like the pointed edges of teeth. She'd bitten him?

Thor let go, dropping the lass to the ground. She scrambled backward.

"Ye're a little animal," he accused.

She wiped at her mouth where a trickle of blood came to the corner. Was it his?

As if sensing his question, she snorted. "'Tis mine. I bit my tongue when ye dropped me, ye no good, filthy son of a whore."

Thor's mood darkened instantly. No one was aloud to talk about his mother. She was a saint in his eyes. The woman had dealt with a blackguard for a husband, suffered through it in order to protect her people and her son, only to be betrayed by the bastard and murdered by his cohort.

The ship grew silent, as the men knew what a deadly mistake Alesia Baird had just made.

Without a word, he reached forward, grabbed her by the hand and hauled her toward him, pinning her against him with one arm around her back.

"That was a mistake," he said low, and cold.

"I dinna make mistakes."

"Ye did this time, lass." Tucked up against him, she slapped him hard in the face.

It stung, but not as much as seeing his pain mirrored in her eyes.

"My mother was not a whore." He kept his voice low, with a level of threat should she decide to continue down this path.

"How lucky for ye," she spat. "Mine *was*." Her words were filled with anguish, and he felt it all the way deep in the center of his body in that dark place where he'd banished any and all emotion.

Thor let her beat him then. Let her wail on him, getting all the anger and pain out pummeling his chest. He could take it. And he wanted it. Needed the physical pain to distract him from the emotional. With his gaze locked on hers, he saw Edgard dismiss the men out of the corner of his eye, allowing the lass a moment of privacy in her anguish. It was obvious she wasn't going to win this battle, but neither would she lose. The men would give their captain congratulations later, but Thor wouldn't take it.

He'd not won this fight fairly. Not when her heart and her mind were so ravaged. And he wouldn't hold her to a week in his bed either. That wouldn't be fair.

"That's enough, Miss Baird," he said calmly.

But she didn't stop, so Thor wrapped his arms around her, pinning her flailing limbs as he'd done in his cabin upon their first meeting. She writhed and grunted until he thought perhaps she was possessed, and then she fell limp in his arms, her face resting against his chest. When she started to shake, he realized she was crying. Sobbing, in fact.

Thor held her, letting her cry against his chest, wetting his shirt, until the skies overhead opened up in solidarity. Rain poured down on them, soaking them to the bone while she sobbed. And still his patience kept. He didn't know why. He wasn't one for emotion, let alone great shows of it. To have a woman weeping in his arms would have sent him running just the day before. Hell, he couldn't stand a blubbering being. He would have left any other to whine and wail on the decking, but Alesia was different. And he didn't know why. There was just something about her.

She was the same lass he'd seen jumping across barrels and taunting the guards at Port of Leith in Edinburgh, and perhaps that was when she'd first garnered his respect.

Ballocks... Respect?

Thor didn't fully respect anyone save Shaw, his pirate prince, and MacAlpin, their king. Even the men of his brethren, though they had his esteem, only held about seventy percent of his respect, the other thirty percent he spent questioning their sanity, guts and intelligence.

All the sudden, he noticed that her sobbing had stopped,

and he looked down to see that she was staring up at him. Her eyes were red and swollen, her lips, too, moist from the rainwater and tears.

He had the sudden urge—nay, *need*—to kiss her. With his gaze on her lips, he slowly lowered his head and then stopped. He couldn't kiss her. That made him no better than any other man that had abused her all her life.

"Dinna stop," she said, and leaned up on her bare tiptoes to brush her wet lips to his.

The touch of her lips on his was soft, tentative, and it sparked something inside him that had him holding her securely to him. Bones and blood, she felt so good. He could have fallen to the deck with her right then and there. But the idea of doing so made him suddenly hesitant. He'd never used caution when kissing a woman in his life. Until now. He wanted to, desperately, but did not want her to believe that he was merely taking advantage of her.

"'Tis a tie," he whispered against her soft lips. "Neither of us won."

"That is not why I'm kissing ye," she said softly, her warm breath fanning over his mouth. "And I willna be asking ye to walk the plank. Take me back to your cabin."

Invitation laced her voice. Was she offering up her surrender?

Could he take her up on it? Hadn't that been his plan all along?

Ballocks, but she had him rethinking all of his plans, his morals.

She was his enemy's daughter, there was no doubt. With her tangle of dark curls, her olive skin tone and seething green eyes, she was the spitting image of her father, though beautiful where the other man was cruel and ugly.

Thor wanted to punish Santiago, wanted to see him in pain.

But was taking advantage worth it anymore?

And was it taking advantage when she willingly offered herself?

Unable to listen to the tumult of thoughts in his mind, Thor lifted her into his arms and hurried them both, soaking wet, back to his quarters.

CHAPTER SEVEN

*O*nce inside the cabin, quite alone and each of them still panting with worked-up breath, Thor set her down.

Alesia stared at him, just a foot, if anything, away from her. He was massive, his scent of sea salt and wind and something else unequivocally masculine and unique to him permeated the air between them.

The scent of Thor.

She wanted to close her eyes and breathe him in, to put a mark on her brain so when they parted ways, which was inevitable, she could remember this moment, remember him.

Captain Thor, whoever he was, and wherever he hailed from, was by far the best man, the best person, she'd ever met —despite him being a pirate. Alesia was a good judge of character. Her entire life, her very survival, depended on it. She trusted her gut. She trusted her instincts more than she trusted another person's opinion or judgment. It was almost as if she had a sixth sense, and that sense had kept her alive. So if her gut told her Thor was trustworthy, she was going to believe it. Without a doubt, he was noble. He possessed a bone-deep goodness she'd never experienced before. One he appeared to struggle with.

That goodness in him made her want to cry at the same time it made her want to leap into his arms and take him up on whatever promise his soulful eyes were making to her just then. His deep-blue orbs were mysterious and mesmerizing, as if he'd seen the bottom of the ocean and had the ability to share the world's secrets with her.

"Who are ye?" she whispered, gulping in the air she needed as her lungs seemed unable to catch up with themselves. She braced her bare toes on the wood planks, feeling her knees knock together. When her fingers started to tremble from the exertion of her emotion, she clutched the sides of her gown.

"I am Thor." The deepness of his brogue, the gruffness of it, stroked along her skin, leaving gooseflesh over her arms.

"Who are ye really, Captain Thor? Ye are not who ye claim to be."

"And yet I've already told ye more about myself than I've ever told another." He took a step forward.

Alesia tried to draw a breath, but it was so hard with him that close. "Where did ye come from?"

"I come from the sea."

Like a merman or some god, she might believe him if he swore it were true. "Not this day, or another day, I mean from the start. Where were ye born?"

He shrugged, ran a hand through his long blond hair. "Does it matter? Does place of birth make us who we are?"

"Perhaps not the place, but the people. Our past does define us, even if we wish it did not."

"And what if I dinna want my past to define me?" He slanted her a challenging glance.

Alesia gave a subtle shake of her head, fisting the gown tighter. "Are we able to make those choices?" She let out a bitter laugh. "Look at me. I am my past. I am my mother's past."

"But not your father's?"

She couldn't meet his gaze as she nodded. "I suppose I am." And that was true, even if she'd deceived Thor about who that might be. Lying to him was getting harder. He'd so readily accepted that she was the daughter of Santiago Fernandez. There'd been hardly any proof needed other than her mother was a whore and she was the right age. Aye, he thought she had similar coloring to the pirate, but if one were to take coloring into account, wouldn't everyone be able to find relation in someone else not of their blood?

Thor wrapped a finger around a tendril of her hair that had fallen loose and lightly tugged until she met his gaze.

"What if we could define who we are despite what forged our pasts? What if we could be whoever we wanted?" His voice was soft now, and she had the urge to sink against him. To wrap herself up in his strength.

"Who would ye be?" Her question was asked earnestly.

"I would be Captain Thor."

"Are ye saying ye've already changed your past?"

"Aye."

"I dinna believe ye. What are ye not telling me?" She'd not meant to ask the question aloud, and yet it had come out all the same. He frowned, dropped her hair and took a step back. Oh, his actions were telling, and so was the tiny pinch in her gut when he did it.

"A pirate never shares his secrets, Miss Baird."

"Neither does a wharf rat." Something in his eyes flickered, and she inched closer to him, dancing her fingers over his forearm and down to his hands, which had so recently been wrapped in her hair. "But there is something about ye, Thor. Something that makes me *want* to share."

The way he was gazing down at her made her belly do a

flip. There was a deep hunger in his eyes that matched her own. His hand beneath hers was warm, of course. They were hands that commanded. That little flip in her belly wound its way lower, sparking a desire in a place she'd never let rule her.

"Dinna confuse a pirate's skill at coercion for anything more."

"Coercion?" A brief smile touched her lips. "I dinna feel controlled by ye."

"Nay?"

"Nay." And that was the truth. Aye, she was in desperate need of a getaway, and he'd supplied both the motivation and the vessel, but with or without him, she'd been determined to leave Edinburgh for good.

There was a subtle shift in his demeanor, as though he wanted to prove her wrong. Did he not realize that she was in control here? Alesia knew the difference. She'd been in situations before where she did not have control. Work-houses. Jail. Even held captive once. What happened to her in those situations was completely out of her own hands, and life had ceased to exist. She knew without a doubt that this was not one of those situations.

Aye, the pirate standing before her was dangerous, deadly even. But she saw beyond that steely façade. She saw his soul. The one that reached out, yearned for another of equal measure. Thor wanted her, not just the physical connection, but her mind. Else he wouldn't still be standing here before her, asking her who she would be, what she would give up. Else he wouldn't have held her while she wailed on him—both with her fists and her tears.

"Does that disappoint ye?" she whispered. "Not control-ling me?"

Slowly, he shook his head. "I admire your strength."

"What else do ye admire about me?" Again, her mouth moved before she had a chance to yank the words back.

"Your will." He stroked the side of her face, running his thumb over her bottom lip. "Your vulgar tongue."

Blood whooshed through her ears, and she had a sudden moment of light-headedness. "Ye'd be the only one."

He cast her a devastating smile. "The rest of the world are fools if they dinna agree."

She leaned into his caress. "I want ye to kiss me."

Thor's pupils dilated, his gaze darkening into an expression of such sensuality she almost melted. But then his lips pressed into a firm line of resolute determination. "I canna."

That was not the answer she'd wanted. Did he not understand how much it had taken for her to ask for a kiss? The one they'd shared on the deck had only been the beginning. She wanted more of those feelings. "Why not?"

"Because if I kiss ye again, I'm afraid I willna be able to stop."

In his eyes, she could see the truth, and she didn't mind it. "What if I dinna want ye to stop?"

The sensual, hungry glisten in his eyes returned. "We shouldna."

"Why?"

He leaned closer, his breath fanning her face. "Because… us together…it canna…" His voice was strangled as his words trailed off.

Alesia didn't want to hear his protests. There was no denying in her heart that she wanted him. There was no denying that he wanted her. They were alone. Why shouldn't they indulge themselves? She wasn't an innocent. Making love wouldn't ruin her. Wouldn't change either of their reputations.

Closing the distance between them, she brushed her lips

over his. He held his lips firmly pressed together, but she felt the warmth. She felt the shift when she continued to press her mouth to his, sensed from the rumble in his chest that he would soon yield. Alesia ran her tongue along the seam of his lips, tasting the decadent flavor of him. She clutched the front of his shirt for balance, afraid that if he did start to kiss her back, she would collapse if she didn't hold on. And then, with a groan of surrender, he opened his mouth and allowed her to invade. Wasn't that a shining victory—the pirate letting her rule?

Alesia was no shy virgin. She'd been with a few men before, some not of her choice. All of them bitter disappointments. She wasn't naïve enough to believe in love, or that providing her body to a man would mean respect or loyalty everlasting. For the most part, she didn't enjoy lying with a man. Didn't enjoy the feel of a heaving body on hers, and most were never kind to her.

But it wasn't like that with Thor. Or at least kissing him led to that conclusion.

The joining of the two of them promised a physical distraction, a moment of being taken from this earth, to feel that maybe she was worth something.

This man, Thor, he made her feel...different. When he looked at her, she had the foreign awareness that he was actually seeing her. That he wanted her—not the pleasure her parts could provide. And that was all the more distracting, alarming, dangerous.

Alesia shuddered as Thor slid a very male hand over her spine. She sank against him, eyes closed, breasts tingling. Tongues entwined, lips of soft velvet pressed firmly to hers. Every inch of her sparked alive with a potent desire that was unfamiliar and entirely too enticing. Thor had the power to keep her right where she was, in this moment, enjoying the hell out of every touch and taste. He moved her hand to his chest, to the muscles there, the pounding of his heart pulsing against her palm. He wanted her to touch him. Her mind, her body wanted so very much to be right here, experiencing whatever this was.

His heartbeat pulsed in time with hers, making the tips of her fingers throb in tandem. With the skill of a seasoned lover, he slid his lips to taste her jaw, behind her ear, the side of her neck. Every inch of skin where his lips and tongue touched was alight with fire, and places quivered inside her that she'd not known existed.

A yearning for more of what he was giving her was incredible and terrifying, and yet she could pull away if she desired—but that only made her want this more. With his teeth, he tugged at her gown just above her breast until her nipple came free. He gripped her hips firmly, massaging as his tongue flicked over the turgid pink tip and his beard tickled her skin.

A moan escaped her. A sound she'd never heard before. A lusty, powerful echo that made her shake and made him groan in answer. Alesia shoved her hands into his hair, holding on for dear life as he laved at her breast. Desire fired between her thighs, sending sparks to lance through her limbs.

Thor murmured something against her skin, but with the blood rushing through her ears, she couldn't make it out. He kissed his way back up to her mouth, hovering over her lips. She blinked open her eyes to find his hazy gaze boring into hers with an intensity that startled her from the fog of desire she'd been fully encased in.

With a curse, Thor pushed away from her, and she welcomed the break from whatever spell he'd put her under. The chance to breathe in cool air and swipe away the shivers. But even distance between them couldn't make the pounding of her heart cease or the tingling quell. If anything, she desired him more. Craved his touch.

Thor ran a hand through his hair, scrubbed it over his face, and whirled to face the wall behind him. He stared up at the ceiling, breath heaving as hard as hers. Alesia felt the need to run toward him and out the door all at the same time.

God, this was confusing.

What was she doing? She tucked her breast back within the confines of the very tight dress. This was not part of the plan. The original or the second. And even if it was part of the third, it was pure insanity. Base desires would not help her true objective.

From the moment she'd climbed onto this ship, the man had been taking her away from her true scheme. Coin. Coin to disappear. Coin to start anew. That was what she needed. Not more fights. Not another man to poke at her parts. Independence. Freedom from a past that kept her firmly rooted in poverty and crime.

But he was not the only one at fault, for hadn't she been just as keen? Well, that was her…mischievous side talking. She needed the level-headed lass back.

A pirate was the last thing she needed. And she should be the last person he wanted to kiss. If he was attempting to return her to the man he believed to be her father, seducing her would only gain the other man's wrath. Was that his plan all along?

A chill swept through her as that realization took root.

Straightening her shoulders, Alesia cleared her throat and asked outright. "What do ye want with me? What do ye want with Santiago's child?"

Thor blew out a breath, muttered another curse. Then he slowly turned to face her, a grimace marring his handsome features. His eyes flashed deadly in the candlelight. "Vengeance." The word came out as ugly as it sounded. It barreled through his gritted teeth to thunk her harder in the chest than it should have.

Vengeance. This was not about returning a child to another pirate who longed to find her. This was much worse. That meant the powerful kiss they'd just shared probably meant nothing to him. Nothing but a way to hurt someone else. She was nothing more than a pawn. And she had no one to blame but herself. She'd allowed herself to get carried away. Thor's true colors were exposed now. He didn't care about harming her, or anyone else for that matter, in order to gain his reward.

"Why? What has that to do with me? I've never met ye before in my life. I've never met *him*. Why hurt me? Why is that the path ye chose?" Despite the emotions whirling and pummeling inside her, Alesia kept her volley of questions even.

Thor's jaw hardened, and she could almost picture the struggle inside him. But that had to be her imagination. She was giving the man too much credit. God, when he'd mentioned coercion, she should have listened. What a fool she was.

"It's not ye I want to hurt, but him."

A shiver of anger ran through her, making her belly hot and her throat tight. Her hands started to shake, and she fisted them at her sides to keep from launching into a physical attack. "The man has not attempted to find me in twenty years. What makes ye think he will care about what ye do to me?"

He walked to a cabinet and pulled out a wineskin, yanking the cork and downing the contents. "Ye're right. The man's a bastard. He willna give a shite what I do with ye."

CHAPTER EIGHT

*T*hor was an arsehole. And he was pirate enough to admit it.

After nearly ravishing Alesia and then telling her it meant nothing but a way to mete out his revenge, he'd stormed from the cabin and refused to lay eyes on her, no matter what she did, for two agonizing days.

When she marched on deck, barefoot, in the too-tight dress and started to climb the mast—he walked away, hooking a thumb over his shoulder in silent demand for Edgard to get her down.

Even when she came up on deck and started to make bets on which of the swabs could take her, he walked away, with Edgard scurrying after to her to diffuse the situation.

At night, when he played his pipes at the bow of the ship, she snuck along the side of the ship, trying to blend in with the shadows to listen. He didn't look at her—but he felt her. Ignoring what he felt was the hardest damn thing he'd ever done.

Each time, he had Edgard take her back to his cabin, lock her in and warn her that if she kept it up, she'd be locked in the brig. The lass never heeded the warnings, and he never made good on his threats. Which of course, made it all the easier for her to drive him mad.

By the time they arrived at Cruden Bay in the north of Scotland, Thor couldn't wait to get off the ship, and away from the lass. Away from the insanity that pummeled him day and night and threatened to toss him off course. Seeing his brethren would help steer him back. The Prince of the Devils of the Deep, Shaw "Savage" MacDougall, was arranging a smuggling deal, here.

"Och, bloody hell," he groaned when he caught sight of the private harbor.

Tucked into the cove were Shaw's ships and two of Constantine Le Breque's ships. Constantine, better known by his friends as Con, was the leader of Poseidon's Legion, the English faction of their pirate brotherhood. Thor had known Con for as long as he could remember. Con and Shaw were very close mates, even if they pretended to hate each other at times. The bond was strong between the two of them. No one, not even a woman, could get between them, though one nearly had years ago. And that bloody *sassenach* could only be here for one reason. The brotherhood was needed, which meant it was very possible Thor's mission to meet Santiago was going to be delayed. Not that he had a burning desire to sail to the pirate town of Puerto de los Dioses on the Azores Islands. Because every moment that had passed since he'd known the lass made the idea of handing her over more and more distasteful.

"Bring *The Sea Devil* in besides the prince's ship," he ordered his men. "Lay anchor and get me a skiff to row to shore."

The men worked the sails, getting close enough to the cove to hide the vessel from anyone passing by, but not close enough to ground them against the sea floor. The *Savage of the Sea*, Shaw's ship, loomed beside them. Powerful and a symbol of their brethren. Shaw's flag matched Thor's, but with a subtle twist. Ruddy in color, their flags boasted a massive ship with the image of a devil's head and a sword-bearing fist crushing it. The difference was Shaw's devil head had a light ring around the top—indicating his crown.

The other ship in the shore, *The Gaia*, was definitely Con's, and beside it, his newly acquired vessel, the *Leucosia*. She was a beauty who rivaled even Shaw's magnificent vessel, since Con had recently had her reconditioned. On the other side of Shaw's ship was *The Dark Sidhe*, captained by Kelly O'Murphy, one of the brothers in the Devils of the Deep. That meant, Lachlan, his other Devils brother had to be at home on their base at Scarba Isle. And if the *Leucosia* was here, Lucifer was traveling with Con.

He climbed over the side of the ship and was about halfway down the rope, ready to drop into the small boat that would take him ashore, when a sharp, feminine voice rang out behind him.

"Move aside," she shouted at the men above, and then he saw her beautiful face as she leaned over the side of the hull and pierced him with a glower. "I'm coming with ye."

Thor growled, meeting her gaze for the first time since their kiss, and he shook his fist at her. "The only place ye're going is back into that cabin." He pointed at Edgard, who started forward, but the lass yanked a blade from behind her back and brandished it at him.

"I said, I'm coming with ye. And I willna hesitate to cut Edgard here, no offense, sir," she said to his first mate, "but I want off this vessel, and I'm willing to fight ye to get there."

Edgard kept his face stoic, but the expression in his eyes when he glanced down at Thor said he was furious—and not at her.

Thor gripped the rope ladder and fairly flew up the half

he'd already descended, flung his leg back over the side and stalked toward her, heedless of the blade glinting in the sun. "Get back in that cabin, or I'll be forced to use the blade on ye meself."

She bared her teeth at him, hand that held her weapon steady. "Put me in that cabin, and ye'll regret it."

He believed her.

Already he regretted so many things. Like the fact he'd not been this close to her in days, and that she was still wearing the same too tight gown and smelled heavenly. His cock, evidently, also could not forget, and began to swell in his breeches as he recalled just what her pink, perky breast looked like, what she tasted like. How she'd offered herself to him.

The woman was dangerous beyond the blood of her father that ran in her veins. Dangerous to his senses, his very thought process.

Gritting his teeth, he grabbed her by the arm, forgetting that she'd ripped the sleeves from the dress. His fingertips came into contact with her bare skin and a spark of lightning jolted up his arm.

"Ye're a pain in the arse," he grumbled.

"Ye havena seen anything yet," she threatened, meeting him head on.

Green eyes blazed, she was so stiff, so ready for a fight that he wanted to kiss her and feel the way she melted against him all over again. Oh, it would be heaven in itself, not to tame her, but to unleash her passion and have it directed at him and at pleasure.

"If I bring ye ashore, ye'll behave yourself." It wasn't a question, but a demand.

She let out a short laugh. "How does one behave themselves when surrounded by pirates?" She stomped on his foot, pain shooting from the bones she'd bruised.

Thor gritted his teeth, cursing softly. "That's the thing ye have to remember, lass, they are all pirates, and not all of them are as patient as I am. I'll not be rushing to save ye when they decide to show ye what they think of a hellion like ye."

That obstinate chin jutted forward. "I dinna need saving."

Now it was his turn to laugh. "Ye have no idea. I assume ye can swim?"

"Of course—" But before she could finish her words, he'd lifted her off her feet and tossed her overboard. She sailed through the air, gown belling out and exposing her pointed ankles and curvy calves. Och, but it was a beautiful sight to behold, and then came the splash as she landed in the blue water that sparkled like diamonds.

Thor sighed as he looked down at her and his handiwork, feeling mighty satisfied at having shown her who was boss. But beside him, Edgard was attempting to give him a piece of his mind. Evidently, while he'd put the man on bairn duty, he'd grown a soft spot for Alesia.

Below, she sputtered in the water, cursing his name and shaking her fist at him. Thor laughed. "Sorry, love, I couldna help myself. My foot feels better now though."

She glowered up at him but ceased her prattle. "Touché."

That made him laugh all the more. What a good sport she was. God, he wanted to tug her from the water and kiss her until they both fell below the depths. Once he was down to the boat, he held out his hand for her. "Come on."

"I think I'll swim."

"Suit yourself. Though 'tis a long way, and soon that gown will drag ye under."

"Maybe I'll just take it off. Besides, seems like the fishes might be better company." Now she was pouting, and her lips were turning a little blue from the cold. But all he could think about was her swimming through the water naked. And everyone else seeing those glorious pink curves.

Nay. Out of the question.

"Och, but it's not as warm," he cooed. "Come on into the boat afore ye freeze to death. I promise to behave."

She didn't argue, though she did mutter a few choice words as she swam over to the side and accepted his hand. He braced himself for balance, and then hauled her into the skiff. Clutching her soaking wet against him, he wrapped her up in an extra plaid, waiting for her to throw a punch. But she didn't.

"Thank ye." Her teeth chattered as she spoke. Dark tendrils of hair stuck to her face like blackened rivulets, and he brushed several away from her eyes.

"Ye need not thank me, lass. It was rather ungentlemanly of me to toss ye overboard." He helped her to one of the benches and sat opposite her.

"Whoever said ye were a gentleman? Besides, I deserved it." Fingers tipped with blue nails from the cold reached to ring out the water from the hem of her gown.

"Nay, ye didna." And he was serious. If she stomped on his foot every five minutes for the rest of his life, he'd consider himself lucky enough to have garnered her attention.

"But I did. I hurt your foot."

He chuckled. "Ye've hurt a lot of things on this ship over the past few days, and while I gained an immense pleasure from dunking ye, it gives me no satisfaction to see ye beaten."

She raised a questioning brow at him and twisted her hair in her hands, sending more water to splash into the bottom of the skiff.

"I've admired ye since before we first met for your…spark."

"Before we met?" She stopped wringing out her gown to stare at him in surprise.

"I saw ye at the wharf." He picked up the oars and started to row toward shore. "Running from the authorities."

She chewed her lip and seemed to sink deeper into the plaid. "I see."

"Dinna be shy with me now, love."

"I'm not." She blushed, and he could only guess what she must be thinking.

Heaven help him, but she was a beautiful woman. With their words at a momentary end, he rowed toward shore as quickly as he could. When they made it close enough to debark, he hopped out and pulled the small vessel the rest of the way to the beach. Then he lifted her and was surprised she didn't protest. Instead, she burrowed closer to him, and he realized just how cold she must have been.

"There'll be a fire inside to warm ye."

She nodded, teeth chattering.

"Dinna become ill. I willna allow it." If she grew sick from his little jest, he'd never forgive himself.

"While I will endeavor to heed your demand, ye do understand that illness is not a choice?" Even with her teeth chattering and her face burrowed against his chest, the saucy side of her never ceased.

"Everything is a choice, lass."

She scoffed. "Stubborn pirate."

"Loud-mouthed wench," he retorted.

Alesia *humphed* and sank closer to him, her slim body feeling entirely too right in his arms. His boots sunk into the pebbly sand of the beach. Ahead of them was a smuggling town run by pirates, built into the caves of the shore. While there were some signs of life beyond the lapping of the waves on shore and the squawks of the sea gulls, it was mostly quiet. It was why they'd chosen the cove for these latest missions, for the revelry that went on inside was barely heard.

On the beach, they were met by the young Xander—whose identity they'd helped erase in order to keep him safe. Months ago, Shaw had been contacted about a treasure that had the power to destroy both Scotland and England. Turned out that the treasure was in fact a lad of royal birth whose enemies wanted dead. Now, under Shaw's protection and with a new identity, the lad was thriving. In fact, Shaw was grooming him to be the next pirate prince.

Thor hadn't seen the lad in a couple of months, and he could have sworn Xander had grown at least two or three inches. He'd filled out and had a good bit of sea sun to darken his skin from all the work on the ships. Thor wasn't surprised they were greeted by the lad first. He'd admired Thor from the moment they'd met and had begged Shaw to allow him to go with Thor on *The Sea Devil*. Shaw had considered it, if only to torture Thor, who didn't enjoy the company of adolescents. Hell, he could barely put up with the swabs who were in their early twenties. There was something about passing the twenty-fifth year of life that put a bit more maturity in a lad and made him into a man. Before that, they might as well still be suckling at their mother's teat.

"Captain Thor," the lad breathed out in exultation. His gaze dropped to Alesia, and color bloomed red on his cheeks.

"Xander. I hope the pirate life is treating ye well."

"More than I dare to say."

Thor grunted, and his men joined them on the beach.

"The prince is waiting." Xander hooked his thumb over his shoulder, indicating the hidden town in the caves, though his eyes never left Alesia. Rotten wee rogue. Holding Alesia with one arm, Thor tapped the lad on the back of the head, jarring him from whatever line of thought he'd been meandering through.

"Lead the way, Xander. Eyes off the lass."

As they began to walk up the beach toward the makeshift

pirate town, Alesia squirmed against Thor and whispered, "Put me down. I'm not an invalid."

Thor kept his gaze ahead, afraid if he looked at her, he'd soften and give away his feelings for her in front of Xander. Not that he was aware of what his feelings were exactly. "Aye, but ye're freezing and soaked."

She wriggled weakly. "All the more reason I should stretch my legs and get the blood flowing back into them."

All the more reason she shouldn't, for blood would be flowing in any number of men's limbs, including his own, when they caught sight of the too-tight gown clinging wet to her luscious body and her hardened nipples jutting from the fabric. He was already rapidly growing hard, proving it would be an extremely bad idea to put her down.

"Thor. Release me," she demanded.

The men who accompanied them slanted curious glances their way, and rather than be seen coddling a female, he relented and set her on her feet. "Your funeral," he muttered, tucking the blanket more fully around her.

"What does that mean?" She walked beside him, clutching the blanket and hiding all the parts he'd been worried others would see. Thank the bloody sea saints.

"Never mind," he growled.

She frowned up at him, but he ignored her.

The closer they drew to town, the more the resonances of revelry broke the silence of the sea. Torches lit up the pirate cove, and the sounds of pipes and fiddles playing accompanied the raucous laughter. Beyond the usual pirate carousing, it seemed like Shaw and Constantine might be celebrating.

"Who is the pirate prince?"

Alesia's question made Thor pause. "I have neglected to tell ye where we are. This is Cruden Bay, a pirate cove we've taken over for the time being. A common ground to meet that keeps our enemies away from our brethren strongholds."

"Brethren?"

"Ye recall the story I told ye of Shaw and his men and how they saved me?"

Alesia chewed on her lower lip. "Aye, I recall. Apologies. I fear, I am…nervous and not remembering quite as quickly. Ye speak of Savage. He has quite a reputation in port."

"There is no need to apologize lass. Aye, Savage, our prince. Ye'll be introduced to him shortly. Though, I'm certain he'll want ye to call him by his given name—Shaw."

"And what is your given name?" She wriggled her brows up at him, teasing.

He winked. "No one has ever known."

"But ye know it, aye?"

"Aye." He nodded toward the ships they'd just come from. "Constantine Le Breque's ship is also out there. He's the leader of Poseidon's Legion, our English brethren. He and Shaw are close mates. My brothers, Kelly and Lucifer, are likely here, too."

"I see."

"Their wives will likely be in attendance."

She wrinkled her nose. "I'm not one for making friends."

He chuckled. "I think ye'll find they are a bit different than what ye're used to."

"I doubt it," she protested.

Thor pressed his hand to the small of her back, hoping to impart some comfort. "Keep an open mind, lass. Ye might be surprised."

"I dinna like surprises." She inched a little closer to him.

Thor grinned. "Let's get ye warmed up afore ye start issuing duels."

She frowned up at him, but there was merriment dancing in her eyes.

Xander had run ahead to announce their arrival. Shaw and Constantine came trolling down the path, with both of his other brothers in the Devils—Kelly O'Murphy and Lachlan MacBeth. The latter of whom he was surprised to see, but equally pleased. The last time he'd seen Lachlan, he'd been sailing north intent on raiding the northern isles. Bumping shoulders with Kelly was Lucifer from the Legion. The man had a murderous dark streak that set Thor on edge, but he was loyal and one hell of a fighter. If Shaw and Constantine trusted him, then why shouldn't he?

"Will they...wonder why I'm here?" she whispered beside him.

Thor grunted. "'Twould only be natural."

"And what will ye tell them?"

"The truth."

She inched closer yet again, giving him the impression she sought his protection or wanted to hide. He didn't blame her. The pirates barreling toward them would be terrifying to anyone who didn't know them, and even more so to those who did.

"Dinna be afeared, lass. Ye're under my protection, and none of them would dare harm ye knowing such."

"All right." She didn't sound in the least bit convinced.

"Thor, 'tis about time ye brought your sorry arse to shore. We've been waiting days for ye."

"There was a delay." He glanced down at Alesia and then cut the men off before they could make assumptions. "The woman. She is...under my protection." Thor glanced about them, keeping his gaze serious.

The men stopped their joshing, eyes moving from Alesia to Thor.

"Let's talk inside," Shaw said with a nod.

Unconsciously, Thor took hold of Alesia's arm and led her inside the tavern that Shaw had erected the first time he'd debarked *The Savage of the Sea*. The main room was filled with pirates and wenches. A blazing fire in the hearth let off the scent of peat and roasting meat.

But this was not the room they remained in. Instead, he led them to a more private room in the back, where Lady Jane, Shaw's wife, and Lady Gregg, Con's wife, sat giggling before the fire. Both of their eyes were immediately on Alesia, who tugged her arm from his grasp since he seemed to have forgotten he was holding her, and went to stand before the fire. The blanket slipped from her shoulders to reveal the state of her gown.

"What have ye done to the poor lass," Jane exclaimed, leaping to her feet. "Ye've torn her gown."

Before Thor could answer to the contrary, Alesia straightened. "I assure ye, Captain Thor has done nothing."

The men behind him snickered, reading much more into her comment than what she'd laid at their feet.

"Then he should still be ashamed for allowing ye to walk around in a gown far too small and without sleeves," Gregg replied, flashing him a scathing look.

Thor tossed up his hands. "The lass did it herself, ye meddling wenches." This was why he'd never gotten himself involved with a female before. All they could do was meddle, meddle, meddle. Alesia seemed to be the only one with a different purpose.

To that, he received a pair of glowering frowns from Shaw and Con. Shaw gave him a punch to the arm. "Dinna speak of my wife that way, else I'll help your shoulders lose the weight of your head."

"And I'll be more than happy to reduce ye to a stump," Con added with a punch to his other arm.

Thor rolled his eyes. "Apologies for calling ye both wenches." The ladies tried hard not to smile as they made eyes at their husbands.

"Och, Thor, ye know we're both every bit the wenches ye say we are," Lady Jane said with a wink at Alesia. "In fact, I've been working mightily hard on becoming just that. Now, introduce us to your…"

"She is my bounty." Thor straightened, vexed that if he said anything else, they'd continue to misread the relationship and embarrass Alesia—and torment him.

"Bounty?" Shaw nodded for them all to take a seat as the door to the private dining room was closed.

"This is Alesia Baird, daughter of Santiago Fernandez."

The room went silent, the eyes of the pirates going crystalline and hard.

Thor passed Alesia a cup of ale and a leg of fowl.

"She is not…acquainted with her father," he said, hoping to cease any ill will some in the room might have toward her at the mention of Santiago's name.

Shaw nudged his wife, who shuffled forward, and Lady Gregg followed. "Alesia, why dinna we leave the men to talk, and ye can come see if one of our gowns…suits ye better?"

Alesia's jaw set, and Thor had a moment of panic that she'd challenge the women instead. Their gazes connected, and she seemed to think better of whatever she'd been about to say or do. She passed him her mug and quit the room with a glower.

"Explain," Shaw demanded, his face devoid of emotion, but his tone saying everything.

"I found Santiago's bastard." The men nodded, having seen the resemblance as immediately as he had himself. "I plan to reunite them."

Shaw narrowed his eyes as did Con, glancing at each other. "Reunite them? Since when do ye do charitable works?"

Thor drank the rest of the ale in Alesia's mug. "Trust me, this is anything but charitable."

CHAPTER NINE

*W*hisked up a back staircase and into a snug bedchamber cluttered with furniture and locked chests, Alesia found her heart skipping beats and her breath labored. She didn't know who these people were or whether she could trust them. Thor seemed to know them well, claimed they were part of his brethren, but what she knew of pirates was they couldn't trust anyone, let alone each other.

And women—ha! She'd been betrayed more often by those of her own gender than men by half. So as soon as the doors were closed, she rounded on both Jane and Gregoria with fists raised, ready for whatever it was they were about to toss her way.

"I'll not be locked up by the two of ye." Her voice came out surprisingly steady despite her lack of breath and over-beating heart.

The two women glanced at each other, seeming to speak silently, which had Alesia all the more on edge. They kept their hands where she could see them, neither of them holding a weapon.

"We mean nothing but friendship," Jane started, arms outstretched as she took a step closer, as though Alesia were a rabid animal that needed to be treated with care. The lady was beautiful, elegant, and spoke with an air of nobility. Her gown was of the finest gold brocade, with violet-colored roses embroidered throughout. Golden hair was piled on her head in neat curls, and her brows slashed with teasing intelligence.

"We know you've no reason to trust us," Gregoria said, her voice a smooth English in contrast to Jane's brogue. She, too, was the epitome of elegance, though the wisps of reddish-brown locks that fell from her braid gave off an air of defiance. She wore a gown of soft lavender silk.

"Do ye think me that naïve?" Alesia shook her head. "Ye know nothing of me."

At that, Gregoria nodded, backing toward a chair and all but tossing herself upon it with an air of casual camaraderie. "You are correct, so why do you not tell us a little about yourself."

Clever lady, Gregoria was. But Alesia was not going to be tricked into giving her any information.

Lady Jane, appearing to take a hint from Gregoria, also backed away. Though instead of retreating to a chair, she stepped to an ornate sideboard filled with crystal glasses and decanters, the likes of which Alesia was certain could only have been in a royal palace before now. Jane opened a jug and poured three cups of dark red wine, passing one to each of them.

Alesia held her glass away from her as though it might be poisoned, but the scent of the wine was sweet, and she longed to take a sip.

"I propose a toast." Lady Jane held her cup up in the air. "To Thor's woman, Lady Alesia."

"I'm not his woman. And I'm not a lady, either."

Jane only smiled, making Alesia wonder if she'd heard her at all.

"I often said the same thing myself when I met Shaw." Jane winked. So she had heard her, she'd just chosen to ignore her.

"I hate to disappoint ye—" Alesia paused and set down the cup without taking a sip, as disappointing as that was. "Actually, I dinna care if I disappoint ye. I am not his woman. I am not a lady. And I plan on leaving. Now."

"Truly?" Jane frowned and glanced at Gregoria. "I could have sworn by the way he was looking at ye that…ye and he were…together. Have ye not kissed him at all?"

At that, Alesia's face flamed hot, traitorous cheeks giving away that she had indeed kissed him. Jane and Gregoria both had identical knowing looks on their pretty, clean faces.

"That's what I thought." Gregoria gave a firm nod.

Anger knotted in Alesia's chest. "We might have kissed once, but it was only in a fit of passion. Nothing more. It meant little to me, and less to him."

The ladies gave her a pitying look. Oh, for heaven's sake. Alesia tossed her hands up in the air. Apparently, it was time to set these ladies straight.

"Look at me," Alesia shouted. "My gown is soaked through because the man tossed me into the water. Would a man who considered me his woman throw me off his ship? In case ye're not clear on the answer, it is nay."

They both sighed as if she'd just said the most romantic thing and eyed each other once more as they sipped their wine.

"Ye're both mad." Alesia turned away with exasperation, feeling quite mad herself. "Whatever's in those cups, I suggest ye dinna drink any more of it."

Alesia walked to the far wall, crossed her arms over her chest and stared at the two ladies who whispered and sighed.

What the bloody hell could they even be talking about? She had the distinct impression it was no longer about her.

"Ahoy, lassies," Alesia said in her best imitation of Thor's voice. "Will ye allow me to leave now?"

The two women were both reposed, relaxed even. They sipped at their wine as if blatantly showing her they would not take her up on her suggestion, and instead, they studied her. Where their seats were situated, she'd have to pass them to get to the door. It wouldn't be any great feat to shove them both out of the way. She could tell by the look of them that she was stronger, and she obviously had her wits about her, which neither of them could claim.

"Why are ye looking at me like that?" Alesia couldn't help but grumble.

It was Jane who spoke first. "I grew up privileged, some would say. Father and mother both nobles. My first husband was quite wealthy and titled. But my life took a turn for the worse. I thought I'd made a good choice, living in an abbey, forcing myself to conform, to be someone I wasn't. Someone I didn't want to be."

Alesia stared hard at Jane, wondering why the hell she was sharing so much and yet so little about herself.

"At any rate"—Jane waved her hand as if she were swatting away Alesia's questions—"what I found was that in order for me to be myself, I had to let go of who I wanted everyone else to believe I was."

Alesia's arms fell to her sides as what the lady said sank in, meaning so much and making so much sense it was exasperating. Oh, she understood completely. Jane saw through Alesia's tough exterior. Through the brashness of her attitude, the vulgarity of her tongue, the strength of her bravado. She saw the vulnerable lass that lurked inside. The one that was desperately besotted.

With a bloody pirate.

A passionate, handsome, strong, sensual pirate.

Well, that would have to be dealt with, wouldn't it?

But of course, because she was stubborn to a fault, Alesia couldn't let the woman know how much her words affected her. So she braced her hands on her hips, gave off her most annoyed expression and said very loudly and obnoxiously, "What in the bloody hell are ye talking about?"

When in doubt, let the anger out. That had always been Alesia's motto, and what hadn't failed in the past, couldn't fail her now, right?

Gregoria laughed. Literally doubled over, nearly spilling her wine, or whatever it was in their cups, as she did so.

"I do so love your expressions," Gregoria exclaimed. "I've not seen so much spirit in a woman since I met Jane."

Dear Hell in a breadbasket, what was Alesia to do now? She was surrounded by a bunch of drunkards, except Jane's expression was serious, which had Alesia wondering if the time the woman had spent at the convent hadn't sunk deeper into her veins than she wanted to admit.

"I'm going to walk out of this room," Alesia said evenly. "And neither of ye are going to stop me."

"On the contrary, my dear." Jane's voice held no nonsense. "Ye're my guest, and it would be most unkind of ye to be rude."

Rude? Again, Alesia's mind whirled.

"I dinna want to be here. And me *escaping* canna be considered *rude*." Had the world gone mad? Or just this part of the world? Or just her?

"I understand that, but ye wouldna be here if ye'd not agreed."

"How do ye know that? Captain Thor could have taken me prisoner. Forced me off the ship and into your strange little pirate town."

"He doesna take innocents as prisoners. Nor does the way he looks at ye give me any inclination that's his desire."

Alesia frowned. "Well, I am allowed to change my mind. Which I have done. I wish to leave."

Jane approached her, less cautiously now. "Then allow me to give ye a new gown afore ye go."

"Ye will let me leave?" Never mind the gown.

Jane shrugged, neither confirming nor denying anything. Well, Alesia would take that as an *aye*, and make her way to the door as soon as she was dressed.

"Besides"—Jane touched Alesia's bare elbow—"ye'd not want to make your escape dressed in less than a harlot's gown."

Less than a harlot's... The meaning was both an insult and a fact all at once. Rather than comment, Alesia simply gritted her teeth and swallowed the harsh and vulgar words that came immediately to mind when she found herself in a threatening situation.

"I am not a harlot."

"I would never have thought so." As she turned away, Alesia caught the look in the woman's eyes—triumph, but something else, something bordering on compassion.

Jane opened up a chest and started to riffle through it, muttering to herself as she studied one gown after another and then finally pulled one from the very bottom. The fabric was dark-blue velvet with silver threading, the kind she'd seen on ladies in Edinburgh. She'd always envied the ladies and their apparent lack of worry. They never had to consider where their next meal came from. Or struggle to put clothes on their backs. The gowns she saw them wear were likely only worn a few times before being tossed into the garbage for someone else to salvage. Was that where this gown came from now? Some lady's toss offs?

"I canna wear it." Alesia longed to don the soft-looking gown, even as she denied herself the luxury.

"Why not? 'Tis the right size."

"I'd rather be paraded naked down Leith Street."

Jane cocked her head. "While I admire your…principles or morality, or whatever the reason is ye would deny yourself proper clothes—"

"I would prefer breeches." Alesia felt her face flame red once more. She pinched the skirt of her ruined gown. "To wear that"—she waved her hand in the direction of the blue gown—"would go against my own…self."

"Self? Do clothes make a self?" Gregoria commented, her leg tossed over the arm of the chair, and a lavender slipper poking from under her own skirts.

Alesia rounded on her. "Aye, they do. That is why the men below, half of them wear a plaid—matching plaids, mind ye— and the others wear breeches. That is why ye think I should change my gown, because I dinna suit whatever ye have decided a lass must be."

"Does this not suit ye?" Jane held up the gown in question. "'Tis beautiful."

"Nay it doesna. And while it may be beautiful, I prefer to wear breeches."

"All right." Jane tossed the gown back into the chest and marched toward the door. She yanked it open and yelled for someone, calling out she needed small breeches and a shirt. "Are ye certain ye dinna want a plaid, lass?"

A plaid? Nay, for to do so would claim loyalty to whomever she wore the colors of, and Alesia refused to swear allegiance to anyone but herself. "Nay."

"Boots?"

"I have my own pair aboard *The Sea Devil*." She bit her lip. "I prefer to be barefoot."

"Do ye never get cold?"

Alesia shook her head.

"Well, we all have our quirks." Jane smiled. "I wish I could be barefoot, but alas, I am so clumsy, I'd probably break a different toe each day."

Alesia sank onto the chest where the gown had been tossed and crossed her arms over her chest. While she wanted to continue sulking, she was finding it hard not to like Jane and Gregoria. Their apparent joy for life and the humor they seemed to find in almost everything was contagious. Plus, they did not judge her for wanting to wear breeches. In fact, they were going out of their way to see that she was comfortable.

"From where do you hail?" Gregoria asked.

"Edinburgh. Born and…" She was going to say raised, but could she truly call her upbringing a raising? Nay. Not in any sense of the word they might understand. "Survived."

Jane shut the door, her arms clutching a load of fabric. "Edinburgh, ye say?"

"Born and survived," Gregoria added. "Quite right. We should all say so much about our childhoods."

"Aye," Jane agreed. The lady's eyes grew misty. "Edinburgh is where I met Shaw."

"Oh? That is where I came across Thor as well." Alesia stood and moved closer to the fire, feeling a little more at ease with the two ladies. "Seems the men spend a lot of time in the city. What's the appeal?"

Jane's lips pinched at the corners. "Besides it being a port?"

"Ah, aye, I suppose I can see that," Alesia said. "Plenty of places to blend in."

Jane's eyes flickered, and Alesia wondered what she could be hiding, but she wasn't brave enough to pry. Gregoria seemed to know and approached her friend to take the clothes and pass them on to Alesia.

"You're welcome to go behind the screen to change."

Alesia took the opportunity to do just that, hearing them whisper and unable to make out any of the words. Dressed, she still couldn't face them. Instead, she leaned against the wall, needing the support of something steady. Seeing, hearing the women confide in one another, the support they showed each other, only affirmed just how lonely she truly was.

There had never been anyone she could confide in. Not even her mother. Before her mother had died, Alesia had spent more time running away from the woman, searching her out in taverns to get her home than receiving any sort of comfort from her.

And the men, Jane and Gregoria seemed to truly admire and love their men. Something Alesia had dreamed of only on the nights when she allowed the bleakness to disappear and a fairy tale to emerge.

"Are ye all right back there?" The voice was Jane's, and she sounded genuine.

Tears pricked Alesia's eyes. Why should they care about her? Why did they bring her into their fold? Teasing her, clothing her, feeding her?

Their sincerity and kindness seemed too much, and yet she wanted to grasp it. To pull them to her breast and declare she wanted to be one of them. But Alesia had only ever known bitterness and disappointment. And who was she to kid herself that she was worth anything more than that? She was a wharf rat. A lowly and disgusting breed. Worthless. The scum of the earth.

"What's wrong?" The sound of Jane's voice had Alesia jerking her head up. She'd not realized that she'd sunk to the floor, or that she'd been crying.

Embarrassed, she swiped at the tears on her face and

scrambled to her feet, only to find herself enfolded in a warm embrace and the scent of flowers.

"There, there," Jane said, stroking her back. "All will be well. Gregg and I will see that no harm comes to ye. Ye're safe with us."

Safe. Practically foreign, the word had taken on new meaning since she'd climbed through the portal in Captain Thor's cabin on *The Sea Devil*. It meant hope.

CHAPTER TEN

"*I* canna believe ye found Santiago's daughter." Shaw sat back in his chair shaking his head. "And ye're a bastard for what ye plan to do to her."

Thor had to admit it had been easier to find Santiago's child than he'd initially thought. In fact, he'd thought it would be a lost cause. But he was wrong. And Shaw was right—Thor was a bastard, a fact he'd reminded himself of a hundred times already. "Planned, man. Emphasis on the past. I dinna plan to seduce her any longer." Thor downed the contents of his ale, hating the censure he was gaining from his two happily married comrades.

"But ye will sell her." This time it was Lachlan who spoke. "For a bit of coin?"

"'Tis not like that," Thor grumbled. "The man is looking for her, and he's willing to pay a high price to whoever finds her."

"But if he sees ye deliver her, he'll never believe she's the one," Shaw said. "His hatred for ye runs too deep."

The men didn't know the half of it. All they knew was that years ago, Santiago had captured Thor and tortured him. He had never told anyone about his mother. About his father's treachery, or why he'd been found alone and seeking vengeance as a lad. Or why their pirate king had tucked him into the fold of the brotherhood like everyone else.

Thor set his jaw and spoke calmly. "My hatred for him is a thousand times worse."

Shaw frowned while Constantine chuckled. "Dinna let your hatred rule ye. When we allow our anger to breach our minds, mistakes happen."

"Aye," Con agreed.

"I'll not be making any mistakes where that bastard is concerned." He'd already carefully crafted exactly how his plan was going to work. "But I need your help."

Constantine and Shaw leaned forward at the table, each of them eyeing him with their own speculative glances before making eye contact with each other, some unspoken message passing.

"How?" Shaw folded his hands in front of him, patiently waiting.

"I'll need a new ship. I dinna want Santiago to see me coming."

"Done. Ye can borrow the *Leucosia*." Shaw flicked a glance at Constantine, mirth in the depths of his eyes that Thor was certain their English brethren did not pick up on. Thor held his tongue, convinced that Shaw being so willing to part with a beautiful ship was not just out of the goodness of his heart, but also part of some bigger scheme. "Con gifted me with it as a thanks for seeing him married to Gregg."

"Nay, you cannot allow him to use the *Leucosia*." Constantine's expression was blank. "You've only just received the vessel. 'Twould be a shame to part with it so soon. I'll give him use of one of my ships."

"Nonsense," Shaw argued, the merriment in his eyes increasing. "The *Leucosia* is perfect. I'd not yet found a purpose for her, and it seems only natural that she should be used to exact revenge on a mutual enemy."

Constantine made a choking sound. "I'm afraid I must insist, MacDougall."

Thor raised a brow. Con only used Shaw's clan name when he meant serious business. What was the deal with the galley?

Shaw slammed a fist down on the table, unsettling the ale mugs, tipping one to the floor and spilling its contents. "Who are ye to tell me or my men what ship they can use? Ye gave up the *Leucosia*. She's mine, and she'll be used however I see fit."

Thor sat back and waited as the argument quickly escalated to the two men scrapping it out on the floor, curses hanging on the ends of their flying fists. The two pirates had a longstanding relationship that often came to blows, but their battles only seemed to strengthen the bond between them. Thor wished he knew what the hell was going on with the bloody *Leucosia*. Why was Shaw so insistent on Thor using it, and Con so insistent that he not?

At this rate, Thor could simply take the *Leucosia* and be on his way before either of the stubborn bastards noticed. After another cup of ale, and the men taking bets on who would win, the two of them finally fell apart, blood trickling from each of their lips and knuckles. They lay on their backs breathing hard and glaring daggers at one another.

Thor stood, kicked his chair back under the table and crossed his arms over his chest, staring down at the two of them as though they were wayward children. "If the two of ye are finished, I'd like to continue discussing my plans."

They groaned, and Con stood and reached down to help Shaw up. "You know, don't you?" Con asked.

Shaw grinned like a fool. "Aye. The *Leucosia* is that stolen

Spanish ship, the *Astorga*. And that's why I think it would be perfect for Thor to use her."

Con snickered. "Why did ye not say so?"

Thor's mouth fell open as he stared at the two men who spoke as though he, along with the others in the brethren, were not in the room.

"Your head was shoved too far up your arse for ye to have listened." Shaw clapped Con on the back.

"I was hoping the jest would last a little longer." Con frowned. "I've not been here more than two days."

Now it was starting to make sense.

Both Con and Shaw continually played cruel jests on each other, and the ship was just another of their wicked tricks. If one didn't know better, you might think the men were enemies, but their support and friendship ran deep. They were brothers in every sense of the word, save for sharing a lineage. Right down to the dirty tricks they played on one another.

"Ye must think me a great fool if ye thought I wouldna realize ye'd not just give me any ship."

Con laughed. "No greater fool than you must have thought me when you gifted me the world's tiniest sword."

"Well, ye know what they say about a man's sword." Shaw punched Con in the chest.

Con rubbed the spot and frowned, muttering, "Gregg would beg to differ with ye."

"Och," Shaw snorted, "'tis only because she's never had a real man."

Before they started to punch each other again, Thor stepped between them. "My plans, ye scurvy pirates, can we get back to them?"

"Selfish bastard," Shaw teased. "What can we do to help?"

"I'm headed to *Puerto de los Dioses*. Santiago will be expecting me."

"That's a bad idea." Con shook his head. "If any of those pirates stepped foot into our territory we'd gut them."

"Aye. This is true," Thor mused.

"What makes ye think he will not do the same? Ye think because ye have his castoff he'll not fire on our ships?" Shaw shook his head. "Ye're smarter than this Thor. Ye're letting your anger get in the way of your sound mind."

Thor ran his hands through his hair and suppressed a frustrated growl. He knew Shaw was right. There'd been a few times when their entire fleet had been able to sneak up on an enemy's port and take them out, but there was a reason Santiago was still a problem. He was smart. And he would never allow them to get close enough.

"We'll have to draw him out."

"How do ye propose we do that?" Shaw asked.

Con poured them all another round of ale.

"Got anything stronger?" Thor asked.

Shaw grinned. "Con's given up anything stronger than ale for a wee bit."

"And why's that?" Thor asked.

Con groaned and rolled his eyes. "Shaw saw fit to send a special batch my way."

"I dinna even want to know what was in that." Thor looked into his mug.

"Let's just say whale isna cheap." Shaw let out a mighty guffaw that had Con threatening to pummel him all over again.

"Listen, I've got a lass upstairs who is the daughter of my greatest enemy. If the two of ye canna get it together enough to help me, I'm going to help myself."

Shaw frowned, all seriousness coming into his countenance. He was the prince of the Devils of the Deep, the leader of their pirate faction, heir to the pirate king. While Thor was often candid with his mate, he'd never been so blunt as to say he'd go off on his own. They were brothers, had been since they were lads, when Thor himself had been fished out of the tide and given a position in their brethren.

"I know," Shaw said softly. "We're with ye, brother."

"Aye," Con agreed.

"Then this is how 'twill go down."

ALESIA SPRAWLED ON HER BACK ON A BED, HAVING SPENT MOST of the evening with Jane and Gregg, only coming down to the main area of the tavern for supper. Thor, Shaw and Con had not been within the tavern, and while her two new friends looked concerned, neither of them voiced it.

Friends. Aye, for that was what they'd become. After Jane had caught Alesia crying, she and Gregg had set about making it their personal mission to make Alesia happy and comfortable, which included sharing the adventures of their past, brushing and plaiting each other's hair, spying out the window when they heard a bawdy song, and then giggling when Alesia told them what some of the words meant. The entire concept of friendship was new to her, but she relished it, cherished it and already dreaded what would happen when she had to leave.

They'd eaten quietly, each of them lingering a little too long over their meals until the brethren pirates started to fall over drunk on the tables—and yet there were still no signs of the three men they were waiting for.

Alesia had continued to peek toward the wooden door, but it had remained firmly shut. Not even a servant had gone in or out. If they were in there, they were shut in. But she had a feeling that the men were not within. They had gone somewhere. She wasn't sure how she knew that, or where the feeling stemmed from, but it was there all the same.

Jane had led Alesia upstairs and showed her to a bedchamber similar to the one they'd been in earlier. It was small but cozy with two chairs before a hearth, a small bed piled high with plaid blankets and a side table. The difference here was that the sideboard was not laden with crystal, and there was no chest full of clothes, nor a screen to dress behind. All the same, it was the first chamber Alesia could claim as her own—even if it was temporary.

Jane and Gregg had said goodnight, leaving Alesia for the night. She'd undressed, donning the night rail Jane had given her, and slipped under the blankets. But sleep did not come. She was worried about Thor. About Santiago. About her future.

She'd been so certain about what she wanted, but now… now she wasn't.

The tavern had quieted, and so had the banter outside her window. The gentle lapping of waves whisked through the shutters. The fire in the hearth had long since died down to embers, but the moon filtered through the slats of the window casing, casting wide silver shafts of light all around her.

Alesia had rarely slept a night indoors, and even more rarely in a bed. She could probably count on one hand the number of times a mattress had softened the way for her bones to rest. She was too comfortable. Aye, *too* comfortable, if that were possible. She wasn't used to it. Maybe that was why she couldn't sleep. Tossing off the covers, she crept to lie before the glowing embers in the fire, curling onto her side and staring at the orange glow. She tugged a blanket over her, unable to get warm ever since she'd gone into the water earlier that day. The water itself had not been so cold, but that had been the turning point between her and Shaw. Not the kisses they'd shared, or the secrets, but that playful blow-back and then the guilt he'd felt over it.

What could be more evident than the fact that she hadn't stolen away as soon as the sounds in the tavern deadened? They were still in Scotland. On the coast. She didn't even need to steal a ship to get away. Climbing up the cliff would be difficult, but she'd scaled buildings in the city before. One could do great things when they put their mind to it.

Alesia rolled onto her back, flopping an arm over her eyes and breathing out a sigh.

How many nights had she slept in an alley with snow falling on her head—flakes melting against her skin and freezing on her eyelashes. Now here she was in the warmth of a tavern and longing for that snow, if only to feel...normal. If only Thor were here. Despite how he turned her upside down inside, she felt like she could be herself around him.

Besotted, she was, aye, but also... she thought it might be something more than that. Was this what love felt like? When one loved another, could they be themselves?

"Where are ye?" she whispered, voicing the thoughts that had been running rampant in her mind all night. Oh, she hated that she cared. She'd made several friends on this journey, but there was only one face that kept her awake at night. She shivered, rubbing her hands over her thighs trying to warm up her skin.

"Why are ye on the floor?"

Alesia startled, looking toward the window to see Thor climbing through. She hadn't even heard him open the shutters.

"What are ye doing?" she gasped, clutching a blanket around herself as though she were naked—which she was not.

Thor grinned, the moonlight shining on his pearly white teeth. "Climbing through your window."

"I can see that, but why?"

"Tavern was locked."

"And how did ye know this was my window?"

"Lucky guess." He chuckled at the same time she snorted. "Truthfully, I didna." His boots hit the floor as he landed, and she was again mesmerized by how tall and broad he was. Instantly, a feeling of warmth settled in her bones—the warmth she'd been searching for.

But that didn't matter, she still had to keep up her façade of shock and pique, wasn't that the game they played? "So ye'd climb through just anyone's window?"

"Och, nay, lass, only yours."

Alesia cocked her head to the side. "What if it had been Shaw or Con's wives?"

He shrugged. "They knew which windows belonged to their wives."

"Ye asked?"

"To be sure, lass. I'd not want to be a dead man."

She raised her brows and leaned back on her elbows. "Well, get out now that ye're in."

Thor ignored her, sitting down on a chair and tugging off his boots.

"Put your boots back on, ye vagrant. I didna invite ye into my bed."

Without looking up, he pulled off his hose. "But it's perfectly vacant as ye've found a place on the floor."

She glowered at him, sitting back up to cross her arms over her chest.

"Have ye warmed up yet from your unfortunate bath earlier?" There was laughter in his tone that she found amusing but also irritating. After tossing his hose, he leaned back in the chair, engulfing the piece of furniture and all but making it disappear.

Alesia swallowed. "As a matter of fact, I have, no thanks to ye." As if to emphasize the lie, another great shiver took her.

Unlacing the ties of his shirt, he slowly revealed his

muscled chest to the moonlight, to her. A sprinkling of gold hair covered the corded flesh. He reached behind him and yanked the fabric over his head. Alesia couldn't help but stare at the wide expanse of his chest. If he looked that good in the moonlight, she could only imagine what he might look like during the day with the sun shining golden on his chest.

"Shall I light a candle, love? All the better to see me with."

"Ugh." She huffed and rolled back toward the banked fire.

His footsteps vibrated the wood beneath her, but instead of heading toward the bed, they drew closer to her until she could feel him standing just behind her. She refused to look, as she was certain this was another trick of his, an egotistical trick to be certain.

Next thing she knew, the heat of his bare chest pressed to her back as he enveloped her in his arms. Oh God, but the warmth of him was sweet heaven. She had to bite her tongue to keep from moaning at the sheer pleasure of it, and she squeezed her eyes shut since she couldn't seem to blink. It was a good thing she had her teeth biting the tip of her tongue, for she was close to asking if he was drunk. No other reason for him to lie here with her this way came to mind, but she detected no scent of alcohol on his breath as he sighed near the back of her head. That slight gush of air scent a shiver cascading over her—and not because she was cold.

"What in blazes are ye doing, pirate?" she hissed.

A low rumble in his chest wound its way around her middle, tickling its way through her veins. "Keeping ye warm."

"I've a blanket for that."

The jerking movement behind her made her think he'd shrugged.

"Am I not allowed to hold ye, lass?"

"Nay!" She stiffened.

"Why not?"

"Why would ye? I'm not your woman."

"But ye could be."

"One kiss, Thor, that was all we shared."

"I believe 'twas two kisses. And they were both verra delicious kisses, were they nay? Perhaps not, since ye didna remember one of them."

Heat flamed her face. They were both indeed delicious kisses. Ones she'd found herself daydreaming about more often than she ought to. But nay. This was not how it could be. Whenever she was near him, her mind and her heart became all jumbled up with ideas she shouldn't have. And even when he wasn't there, they still did the same.

There was nothing for it. Alesia needed to stick to her plan, or else she'd see her heart broken. And considering she thought she might love him, leaving him here would make it painful all the more. But it was better than the alternative—hanging from the gibbet—wasn't it?

The fact that she couldn't even answer that made her bite her lip.

Clearly, she had to leave. Loving Thor would be dangerous for them both.

She still had to plan her escape, and if she were to allow him to continue whatever it was he was doing, she was certain to change her mind by convincing herself there was more to it than there truly could be. Her head started to hurt with the jumble of thoughts once more attempting to make their case.

His arm held her tighter, as though he could hear her thoughts.

"I'll not ravage ye unless ye ask," he crooned. "'Haps it is I who is cold."

"Build up the fire then and get into the bed. Pile on a thousand blankets if ye must, but leave me to my peace." Her voice choked on the last word. Peace was foreign to her.

Except now with his arms around her. Again, the forbidden tempted her to hope.

"That is the thing, my wee rat. I canna seem to leave ye." He sighed, his fingers tracing a circle on her belly that had her sucking in a breath. "So where does that leave me?"

"Lonely."

He chuckled, again the rumbling of his chest to her back marking her. "Och, Miss Baird, but have I told ye how much ye amuse me?"

Her heart did a little flip. "I canna imagine that I care."

"But ye do." He gripped her wrist, pressing his fingers to her pulse point. "I can feel it."

She yanked her wrist away, annoyed that he'd been able to figure her out. "I am more than my baser instincts. Unlike some people in this chamber."

"So ye admit it." There was more than a hint of humor in his tone.

"Of course. I'm not so mysterious."

There was a long pause, and she swore his heart thudded harder against her back. And then he murmured against her ear, "Let me pleasure ye."

Well… Her throat went dry. It seemed every nerve in her body leapt toward him, shouting aye. But nay. She could not. Even if she wanted to desperately. She was falling too deep for Thor. Way too deep. Too late, she made the mistake of pushing her backside roughly against him in an attempt to shake him off, but he only groaned and clutched her tighter.

"Careful, lass."

"Go away."

"If that is what ye truly wish. But some days from now, we will part, and I shall never see ye again. Let us make a memory together."

He made a convincing argument. In fact, she'd used the very same one. Which only bolstered her decision to deny him. "Do ye know how many times I've heard a sailor or pirate say that to a whore in Edinburgh?"

He was silent for a few moments as that sank in, and then he shifted away from her a little. "So does that mean ye wish to role play?" His tone had grown lighter, teasing. And despite what he was suggesting—or the lack thereof—she couldn't help but smile.

"Ye're a pig."

"Aye, perhaps I am. But at least I mean to give more than I receive." There was humor in his voice that made her smile.

"Go to sleep."

"As ye wish, my wee rat." He tickled her belly, making her draw in a breath she wished didn't show how much she actually liked him touching her.

"And stop calling me a rat. And stop tickling me, too."

Thor rolled onto his back, tugging her with him so that her face was now plastered to his bare chest. He smelled good. Felt wonderful. It was a wonder she was able to keep herself from drooling and hold on to her conviction to not kiss him, to not allow him to pleasure her.

"Goodnight, Miss Baird."

"Goodnight, pirate scum."

He chuckled, the rumbling doing things to her insides that seemed impossible. But still, she didn't pull away. She snuggled closer and closed her eyes, feeling more relaxed than she had in days. At the same time, she felt like her limbs would come alive, forming a mind of their own.

This was going to be a very, very long night.

CHAPTER ELEVEN

or the next three days, Thor met behind closed doors alongside Shaw and Con. Lachlan, Kelly and Lucifer acted as messengers between them and the Spanish, using an informant that their brethren had acquired over the years to deliver messages to Santiago. Their go-between was a witch doctor on the Azures Islands that the Spanish pirate captain sought out for the strange pains in his head. And whom Lachlan had once beheld as a lover.

Secretly, Thor thought Lachlan might still harbor feelings for Mari. When this business with Santiago was over, Thor was going to suggest Lachlan give it another go.

Finally, it was settled upon that in two days time they would meet at dawn at a specific latitude and longitude coordinate, roughly equal distance from Santiago's home base as it was from the Devils of the Deep's home base of Scarba—as they didn't want the men to know of their hideout in Cruden Bay.

Once there, they would make the exchange. Alesia for a chest of gold. Though that wasn't truly the goal, only the surface plan that Santiago was aware of. Once they'd attached their grappling hooks to his ships, Thor would let out a call to battle. He would take the man down for what he'd done. Take his life, his gold and his daughter.

Every night, rather than come up the stairs, he climbed through the window of Alesia's bedchamber and curled up beside her on the floor to keep her warm. He didn't try to kiss her, didn't try to touch her in a way that could be misconstrued as anything other than protector. They shared warmth and comfort. And even when she was asleep, she snuggled closer to him.

It was a torment to pull her into his arms and *not* kiss her, but he'd made a promise not to. However, that didn't mean he wasn't struggling something fierce with his desire to both protect her and give her the pleasure he so very much wanted to share. He'd teased her before, played with her, but he did indeed desire her.

More than desired her. For what other woman would he ever have treated thusly? None. There had never been anyone like her. And he believed wholeheartedly that there would never be another as fine.

Aye, she was a hellion to be sure. Perhaps even slightly mad. But weren't they all? Wasn't he?

She was perfect for him in every sense of the way. He only wished that she would open up to him more. To tell him what it was she truly desired. He could sense that though she remained with the brethren, there was only a thin thread keeping her in place. Alesia was used to running, used to having to protect herself, to take care of herself no matter the cost. Hell, that was why she had a price on her head in Edinburgh.

That was why she'd challenged him and every swab aboard the ship to a fight. He was fairly certain the only reason she hadn't challenged those at Cruden Bay was because she wanted to make a good impression on Jane and

Gregg, which meant she must have respect for the two women. Liked them, even. He might even go so far as to say she'd made friends. Surprising, truly, for Thor would have bet a chest full of gold that she respected no one, and only half-heartedly respected herself.

Lying beside him now, the even breaths of sleep he'd grown used to gave off a subtle shift as she woke.

"Ye're still here," she teased, the same thing she said each morning when they woke.

He glanced down at her where her head rested on his shoulder. Beautiful, brilliant green eyes shone up at him, and a sleepy smile curled her lips.

"Ye threatened me in your sleep," he jested back, letting his hand fall from her back as she sat up.

"Ye did well to heed my threats, pirate. I am feared in some parts of Scotland."

"Aye. And perhaps even on the high sea."

She turned to look at him quizzically. "What do ye mean?"

"Ye did come at me, fists of fire on my ship. It's a wonder my men still follow me, as I should have decked ye, tied ye to the mast and beat ye for your insolence."

She laughed, relaying to him the truth he'd known since he'd first spied her in his cabin—she wasn't afraid of him in the least.

After standing and splashing water on her face, she gestured toward the door. "Go on now. I need to make use of the chamber pot."

Thor studied her for a moment, taking in the bare toes and the billowing white night rail tied all the way to the neck. Even looking like she wore a ship's sail, he could watch her all day. He cleared his throat. "When ye're done, prepare to leave. We board the *Leucosia* today."

She paused, wiping her face on a strip of linen. "Not *The Sea Devil*?"

"Nay. Kelly will captain my ship for the interim."

Alesia set down the damp linen and started to comb her fingers through her unruly hair. "Where are we going?"

"Deep into nowhere." Thor stood and began folding up the blankets and tossing them onto the mattress.

"That sounds dangerous."

"Ye like a bit of danger."

"I do. So I am to come?" A hip popped out to the side, giving him a momentarily silhouette of her figure.

Thor forced his eyes back to her face. "Aye. We are meeting Santiago."

Her pallor faded, and she nodded, no longer having anything to say, her jaw gone tight.

Thor wanted to comfort her, but what could he say? For all she knew, he was going to present her to her father, a man he'd told her was a vile heathen, before walking away.

But there was no way in hell he could leave her. How to tell her that though? How to ask her if she wanted to remain with him? So he nodded, lips clamped closed because he didn't know how to form those words in a way that would make sense.

"I'll see ye below stairs," he muttered and then quit her chamber.

In the tavern below, the swabs had formed lines as they carried supplies to the various ships. All the joviality of the days past had ceased as they readied themselves for what could be an epic battle upon the high seas.

"I want Shaw's rum," Con was shouting. "Not whatever you have in those barrels."

Shaw chuckled and waved at the men to do as Con instructed, which had Thor wondering if he'd known that would be the case all along and had tainted his own rum, or if Con was simply paranoid about the last barrel he'd drunk.

"I want to join ye." Wee Xander approached, his dark hair having grown long and a faint, youthful mustache feathered on his upper lip.

"Nay." Thor took a stone to his sword, sharpening the edge as he watched Edgard give orders to his men.

"But why not?"

"Ye're with Shaw, lad."

"But Savage is so…strict."

Thor leveled a glower on the lad as he ran the stone down the length of the sword hard enough to create sparks. "What makes ye think I willna be just as strict?"

Xander tapped his chin and rolled on the balls of his feet, a smile of triumph on his face as he said, "Because ye're Thor."

"And?"

Xander frowned. "The men on your ship are allowed to walk around in any state of dress they please. With the lady on board, I have to wear breeches. I'm not even allowed to wear a plaid."

Och, leave it to a green-faced lad to bring leadership down to such a low level as his state of dress.

Thor glanced over to where Shaw stood with his wife, Jane. The lady smiled up at Shaw the way Thor wanted a lass to smile at him. But not just any lass—Alesia.

"Why are ye not allowed to wear a plaid?"

Xander's face reddened. "On account of me accidentally mooning the lady when I meant to do so to one of the swabs."

Thor held back a chuckle as he imagined Xander tossing up the back of his plaid and his arse turned in Lady Jane's direction. Och, what he wouldn't give to have seen Shaw's reaction.

"Besides, Savage never shares his haul of crab, and I am fond of crab." Xander turned to the sea, perhaps pondering whether he might go down to the rocks to find a crab or two crawling between the crevices.

"Do ye want all the crab, lad?" Thor bit the inside of his cheek to keep from laughing as he asked.

"I do." Xander nodded resolutely.

"Then ye'd best stick with our prince, for he is grooming ye to follow in his footsteps. Then ye shall have as much crab as ye wish."

"Aye. That is why he is so strict, I suppose."

"I will not be any less strict. And I'll not have my arse handed to me for catering to your adolescent quibbles. Go away."

"Aw, come on, Captain Thor." The lad ducked his head, shuffling his feet. He was perhaps fifteen summers and feeling the barriers of his seclusion. Since he was a wee bairn, he'd been hidden away from view, the threat of death over his head never vanishing. Born a prince—the rightful heir to the Scottish throne—and presumed dead, he'd been hunted until just this year when Shaw swept him right out from under the noses of those who might be looking for him. And now Xander could likely taste freedom, although it wasn't his to grasp just yet.

"I canna go against our prince, and ye shouldna be asking me to. I'll keep this between us, because I know what 'tis like to be your age and conforming to the rules, but if ye ask me to go against Savage again, I'll be forced to tell him."

The lad's face went white. "I willna, I swear it."

"Good. If ye're looking for change, ye know the prince is always willing to lend an ear, aye?"

Xander reluctantly nodded. "Run along then, and do as he bid, else we both incur his wrath."

The lad ran off, leaving Thor to think about another person who wished for freedom.

ALESIA STOOD AT THE BOW OF THE SHIP, WATCHING THE pirate's cove slowly disappear into the distance. The vast sea, wide and terrifyingly unfamiliar, lay sprawled out to her back. The only home she'd ever known had been Edinburgh. Now, in the span of a sennight, she'd been to the northeast of Scotland, and was now headed to the middle of nowhere in a vast expanse of water. Nowhere to swim if their ship should sink. Nowhere to escape.

Nay, the time for escape had passed as soon as she'd climbed the ladder from the skiff onto the ship. What had made her do it?

Every night when Thor climbed into her window with ease, he'd shown her how simple it would be to escape, and yet at the same time, he'd shown her something else—protection, kindness, companionship.

Had she not escaped because she hoped there could be something between them?

She liked to believe she wasn't so naïve. But here she was on his ship, anticipating the night when he would once again curl himself around her while they slept.

And would he? When she'd slept on the ship before, he'd not come to her. She had no idea, in fact, where he'd slept, or if he'd slept at all.

The quartermaster was shouting orders, and the men were leaping about the ship, tugging at the rigging. They started to sing a song she'd heard many a time at the wharf. A sailor's song that made her smile.

They were so excited to be heading back out to sea, none

of them seeming to experience the angst she felt so deep in her bones.

"What are ye thinking about?" Thor slid up beside her.

"Shouldna ye be at your helm?"

"Edgard's got it."

The *Leucosia* had much the same layout as *The Sea Devil*, although it was slightly smaller and the wood a little more worn.

"Ye take good care of your ship," she mused.

"Aye. Kelly will take good care of it, too."

She skimmed her fingers along the wood of the rail, and stared over the side at the way the water foamed as the ship pushed through it. "Ye're lucky to have men in your life like Shaw, Con and Kelly."

"I've more than that. There's Lachlan and Lucifer, and all the others, too."

"A family." Her shoulders sagged. That was probably one of the biggest reasons she'd found it hard to run. The people she'd met, the friendships she'd formed, were the closest thing to a family she'd ever had.

"A brethren," he corrected.

"Are they not the same thing?"

He crossed his arms over his massive chest, drawing her eye to the thick muscles beneath his shirt and the V of skin that showed where his lacings had come loose. Thor was bronzed with a sprinkling of light hair on his chest that matched the long locks on his head. She longed to reach forward and press her palm over the exposed skin. To lean in close and smell the salt on his skin. To lick that dip at the base of his throat and find out if he tasted as delicious as he smelled.

"I suppose they are." There was a change in his tone.

She jerked her gaze from the strip of exposed skin back to his ice-blue eyes. "I hate to admit it, but I am jealous." She laughed softly at herself and flicked her eyes back toward the water.

"Soon ye shall be reunited with your father."

A shiver of trepidation and true fear slithered over her spine. She had no idea if Santiago Fernandez was her father. He would likely ask her the name of her mother, and as soon as he found her to be a fraud, she'd be cut from stern to groin, the divided pieces of her fed to the fishes.

"I am nay certain I..." She swallowed around the hard lump that had formed in her throat. How could she tell Thor she didn't want to go through with it? He'd arranged this entire thing. He would never forgive her for lying, for making a liar out of him...

"I understand your hesitation," he started and touched her hand where she held firmly to the bow when she tried to interrupt. "But what reason could he have to seek ye out, to pay a reward for ye, if not because he wanted to be reunited?"

"What if he doesna accept me?" She couldn't look at him for fear he'd see the truth in her eyes. *What if he kills me instead?*

"Why wouldna he?"

Oh, she had plenty of answers she could give him for that. All of which might see her to a more timely death than the one she was drifting toward.

Oh God...

Her knees buckled. She was probably in jeopardy of fainting, or at least of tossing up her accounts.

"I need some...water. To lie down." She pressed her lips together, holding back the nausea.

Sensing her sudden illness, Thor scooped her up in his arms and carried her to the cabin, shouting for ale and sweet almonds.

"A little spirits and sweets ought to help perk ye up."

120

She buried her face against his chest. Oh, but he smelled just as she'd known he would. That familiar, comforting sea salt and spice.

The right thing to do would be to confess now, before they got too far away from port. To give him a chance to turn around with his men and call it off.

But she was a coward.

For the first time in her life, she couldn't fight this. She couldn't protect herself. Couldn't protect Thor, or his brethren. They were all in grave danger. And it was all her fault.

She'd gotten herself into this mess and she had no idea how the hell she was going to get herself out…

CHAPTER TWELVE

*T*hor might not be as connected to his emotions as some men, and perhaps there were more than a few people in his past that would say he had a lump of steel where a heart should be. But when it came to Alesia, he found himself in tune with her. However odd or out of place it was, he couldn't deny it.

Clutching his shirt, she trembled in his arms as he entered his cabin. He shut the door and leaned against it with her still curled into his chest. The way she clung to him was not unlike the way he clung to her.

There was no denying it, the moment he'd first seen her running on the dock, he'd known there was a matching spirit inside her. One that spoke to his own.

And she was hiding something. He could feel it. At first, it had been a tickling inside his brain, and now it was a full on assault.

"What are ye hiding, lass?" His voice came out low, gruff.

She jerked against him, but he'd been expecting that, so he held on tightly, walked to the nearest chair and sat in it, the wood creaking from his mass. He arranged her over him, not letting her go, and pressed his nose to her hair. She smelled like sunshine and flowers.

"I'm not hiding anything." But even as she denied it, he could hear the lie laced in her words.

"Let us not bandy about with words, Miss Baird." He twirled a tendril of her hair around his finger. "There is one thing I know, and that is when someone is lying. And ye… well, I seem to know how ye feel even when ye try to hide it."

Their eyes connected, both of them serious. "Then stop looking."

"I confess I've tried, but I canna," he whispered.

She tucked her face back against him and then suddenly shoved away with a growl under her breath. The struggle within her was intense, and he wished more than anything he could help her alleviate it. With his arms wide, he waited for her struggle to end, for her to decide whether she wanted the comfort of his arms, or the solidity of the floor.

Evidently, she chose to remain on his lap.

Eyes on her, no judgment in his tone, he said, "I'll not be angry with ye."

"Aye, but ye will." This time, she did scramble away.

Thor watched her cross the room, lean against the wood planked wall and cross her arms over her chest. She looked everywhere but at him.

"I am not normally a patient man, but I'm willing to make an exception for ye." Where the hell had that come from? Bloody fool he was. He might as well hand her a sword and present his neck.

"I wish ye'd stop being so nice to me." She blew out a puff of breath in an attempt to clear her unruly hair from her face. It didn't work.

"I am not being nice. I am being…" What was he being? For nice was a probably a damned good description of it. "Diplomatic," he decided to go with. "Ye're the daughter of

Santiago. I am conveying ye to him, and so I must make certain ye arrive in one piece."

She snorted. "That's where ye're wrong, Thor."

"Oh? Ye'd prefer to be delivered in pieces?"

"Might as well." She tossed her arms up, exasperation in her tone and creases in her brow.

To say he was confused would be an understatement. "Explain."

"Neither of us have proof that I am who I say I am."

Thor narrowed his eyes, stood from the chair but did not approach her. "What is your meaning?"

"I could be lying." She started to pace, a telltale sign that she probably was in fact lying.

"Ye could."

"And ye"—she jabbed her finger at him—"would risk both our lives?"

"Where is this coming from?" Thor crossed his arms over his chest, trying to sort through her words and expressions to figure out what the bloody hell she was talking about.

Her pacing increased, and he feared she may get a splinter in one of her tiny pink toes at the speed she was going. "Santiago, if he's as ruthless as ye say he is, he could believe I'm not his child, that this whole thing is a ruse and ye, and your men could be killed."

The very idea that she didn't trust him to keep her and his men safe was a worse punch to the ballocks than the one she'd given him upon boarding his ship. "Ye dinna have faith in my ability protect me and my men? To protect ye?"

"I dinna know ye." Suddenly, her pacing ceased, and she pursed her lips.

This time, Thor did move. He crossed the cabin in a few strides and caged her against the wall with his arms. "Ye know me, lass."

Their eyes locked, breaths heaving, mingled. Her chest

rose and fell with speed against his own. God, he wanted to kiss her, to remind her that he knew her. That he knew her better than anyone else.

"Ye dinna know—"

He cut her off. "Aye, I do know ye. I know ye're stubborn and full of fire. I know ye've a mean right punch, and when backed into a corner ye'll resort to nasty tactics." He crossed his knee up over the other, blocking the blow she meant to his manhood. "Just like that. I know there's passion in ye. Loneliness, too. Dinna say I dinna know ye, for I know ye better than anyone else."

"Am I so obvious? So plain? So thin that my insides seep like sieve?"

"Nay."

"Dinna lie."

"I'm not. I know ye, because I am like ye. Because in ye, I see a part of myself."

She snorted. "Ye see a means to exact your revenge. Dinna think for a minute I dinna know exactly what ye mean by giving me away."

"I'm not giving ye away."

Beautiful green eyes squinted in question at him. "I implore ye, Thor," she said, her voice hoarse, "if ye know me so well, dinna trifle with me. I am more fragile than I look."

"I know." He pressed his body against her, unable to help himself from getting closer. Blood pooled in his groin, and he longed to make her his.

She was more potent than the finest spirits, more addictive than seeking treasure.

A tear rolled from the corner of her eye, and he brushed it away with his thumb. Ballocks, but he wanted to kiss her. To show her with his body just how much she meant to him. What was this feeling coiling hot in his chest? This need to absorb her?

"Tell me your true name," she whispered. "If ye really mean all the things ye say, tell me what ye've never told anyone else."

Without hesitation, he spoke, "Thornley MacLeod."

"Thornley." The way she said it, so smoothly on her velvet tongue, had him melting inside.

How many years had it been since he'd heard someone speak his name? Not since he was a lad. When he'd been found by the king of the Devils of the Deep, he'd only given the man his nickname. "Thornley is dead, love. I am only Thor now."

A tiny warm hand pressed to his heart. "He is there. Right here, hiding. He shapes ye. Just like everything I wish I could forget shapes me."

Why did what she say have to make so much sense?

"I have to confess. Before 'tis too late." She glanced down at where her hand pressed to his heart. "I am not Santiago's daughter."

"Ye are."

"Nay." She shook her head, sadness turning her lips downward. "I'm not."

"Ye're only saying that to get me to turn the ship around. Ye're afraid to face your past."

She shook her head. "Nay, ye're not listening to me, Thornley. I lied."

There she went distracting him by saying his name. "What do ye mean?"

"I wanted the coin to start a new life. They were going to hang me in Edinburgh. I needed to escape." She shrugged. "Boarding your ship and pretending to be someone I was not was the simplest way to get out of the port and gain some coin in the process."

"Do ye know the identity of your father?"

"Nay." Her fingers played with the ties of his shirt.

126

"Then how can ye say for certain it is not he?"

"Because I dinna believe in coincidences."

"Lass, did ye ever wonder why I believed ye? Why the men of the brethren believed ye?"

She looked up at him startled. "Aye."

"Because ye look like Santiago. Ye have his hair, his eyes. Ye have his mean streak." Thor couldn't help but add this last part with a chuckle. "I believe ye're his. And so does everyone else."

"I canna risk your lives."

"By doing what? This is who we are, lass. Even if I knew for certain ye were not his daughter, I'd still be sailing to the meeting point. A chance to gut Santiago has always been my mission."

"And what if I am his daughter, and I dinna want ye to kill him?"

"Is that what ye want?" He stared intently into her eyes, realizing that if she asked him not to, he wouldn't go through with it. "I could just take a limb, or an eye, if that is what ye wish."

"Why do ye hate him so much?"

Thor told her about how he'd been taken prisoner by Santiago some years back. Tortured and tossed into the sea to be eaten by sharks. He didn't share with her about his childhood. "I escaped."

"On the backs of dolphins?" she asked skeptically.

"Aye."

"Impossible." She rolled her eyes.

He grinned. "Living proof."

"I'd have liked to see that." She was pinching her lips, trying not to smile.

"Maybe ye will. Maybe I'll do the same to him."

"So ye're saying this is simply an eye for an eye." Her pert nose wrinkled. Something must have flickered in his gaze, because she narrowed in on him, intelligence sparking in her eyes. "'Tis more than that."

"Would ye have me bare my entire soul to ye, lass? I've already told ye my name."

"I'd never ask anything ye werena willing to give."

"And what about ye? I've told ye something no one else knows. Tell me something. What is your deepest, darkest fear?"

She chewed her bottom lip, looking over his shoulder as she searched her mind for something to share. "I fear I will die without knowing love. And I dinna just mean the love of a man." A sad smile crossed her lips. "I never knew the love of a mother or a friend, either."

Thor's heart might have broken at that moment. Aye, his family, his entire world, had been ripped from him, but in its place, he'd been given a new one, his brothers. Without the brethren, where would he be?

Leaning close, he pressed his lips to her forehead, breathing in her light floral scent. "Santiago... He ruined my life."

She wrapped her arms around his neck, and pressed her lithe body tighter to his. "He took life from ye and at the same time he gave it to me," Alesia whispered, her lips pressed to his chin. "Maybe there is such a thing as coincidence."

Thor pressed his lips to hers, kissing her softly. "Whether there is or isna, I'm glad ye snuck aboard my ship." He traced the line of her jaw with his fingers.

"Me, too. But where do we go from here?"

"Do ye still want to escape me?" There was a hitch to his tone that he knew was a telling sign he hoped she'd say nay.

There was a long pause as she struggled. He started to back away from her, allowing her any space she might desire, but she held on to him tighter. "I dinna. That is why I boarded this time, too. I had plenty of opportunities to run at Cruden Bay, but…something held me back."

"My life is dangerous. Ye were trying to leave that behind."

"I feel safer with ye than I've ever felt in my entire life."

He gathered her back in his arms, vowing to never let go. "Saints, lass, but I feel the same."

She laughed. "Was it my right hook?"

"Something like that."

Alesia laughed harder, her head falling back, tendrils of her unruly hair coming loose from her braid and tickling his arms. Thor was pretty certain he'd never seen a woman so beautiful in all his life.

Without thinking, he pressed his lips to her exposed throat, drinking in the soft gasp of pleasure she emitted.

"I'm sorry, lass, I couldna help it."

"Dinna apologize. I want ye to kiss me. To show me…pleasure."

At last. How long had he waited for this moment? "Och, but I'm certain I've never heard a more enticing request." He kissed her neck again, tracing a line with his tongue up the column to her jaw, where he nipped gently.

"How do ye make simple things so amazing?" she whispered.

"I dinna, sweet lass. But together, we do. Together we are fire." His mouth sought out hers, and he could have sworn a spark lit between them.

Alesia tangled her tongue with his as they wrapped their arms around each other. Their kiss had begun soft, languorous, but just as quickly as a fire could leap into a mighty inferno, so did their fervor. As their mouths dueled and pleasure ignited, they tore at each other's clothes. Thor walked them backward, dropping garments until they were falling onto the mattress naked.

She straddled his hips, her beautiful creamy skin exposed to him, tight, perky breasts tipped with twin cherry nipples. Thor was certain he'd never been more full of desire. It seemed right for her to be leaning over him. To give her the power over whatever went on between them.

He ran his finger from the dip at the base of her neck down between her breasts, watching her suck in a breath, the muscles of her belly tightening. Subtle bruises marred her flesh. Some fresh purple, some yellowed with age, a testament to the rough life she'd led.

Leaning up on elbow, he kissed each one and told her he would kill every last person that left a mark on her. She sighed, her fingers running through his hair.

"My beautiful, Alesia," he murmured against her skin. "I want ye. Will ye let me have ye?" He gazed up at her, eyes locking.

Alesia leaned down low, pressed her lips to his and whispered, "Ye had me from the very beginning."

Och, holy hell, he was going to make love to her, and he was pretty certain it would be the end of life as he knew it.

CHAPTER THIRTEEN

*I*n all her life, Alesia had never felt any semblance of power. But with her body suspended over the muscular giant who stared up at her with such potent hunger, she felt like she was the most powerful woman in all the world.

She'd not been lying when she said he'd had her from the very beginning. The moment he'd ducked beneath the cabin door, and she'd stood there with seawater pooling at her feet and caught sight of his glittering blue eyes, the mischievous smile, he'd struck a nerve inside her.

She ran her finger down the wicked scar along the side of his face and tugged on the hair covering his chin.

"Does it bother ye?" he asked.

"All of ye bothers me," she said with a teasing smile. "My body tingles whenever ye look at me, and when ye touch me." She pulled his hand to her breast, her head falling back on a sigh as he stroked the pad of his thumb over her nipple. "I feel like I could fly."

Thor leaned up on his elbow, his hot breath on her breast drawing Alesia to look down. She watched with fascination as his tongue darted in and out from between his lips to flick over her skin. Her nipple tightened at the touch, reaching for him. With every lick, a spark shot from her breast and arrowed down between her legs.

Men had used their mouths on her breasts before, but never had it felt like this. Her breath hitched as his tongue darted but then paused, hovering just a hair's width from her straining flesh. Oh God, why did he tease her so? She waited, breath held until he finally swirled the velvet tip around and around and drew her nipple into his mouth.

How was she going to be able to hold herself upright when all she wanted to do was fall? Alesia threaded her fingers into his hair, widening her thighs over his hips, trying desperately to anchor herself somehow, when in her veins flowed liquid gold.

"Ye like this." It wasn't a question he asked, but a statement as he slid his mouth to her other breast to pay it equal homage.

"Aye," she moaned with wonder.

"Ye sound surprised." *Flick. Swirl. Suck.*

Alesia could barely form words around her hiss of breath. "Everything about ye surprises me."

"Oh?"

"Aye." She tugged at his hair and instinctively rolled her hips, pressing the heat between her thighs down onto him, searching for... Ah, aye, there it was.

Thor's firm, swollen length answered her searching touch and pressed unyielding to the softness between her legs. Alesia couldn't help but moan and grind against his thick arousal again. And again, it felt so good. What was this sparking pleasure, this delicious heat that spread through her?

Large fingers gripped her hip, his thumb pressing to the bone and the rest of his fingers spreading over her flesh, searing her, branding her. "Gentle, lass, else it is all over before we've really begun."

"How do we make it last?" she asked, not wanting it to stop, but knowing from past experience if a man was as hot and bothered as Thor was, he would soon be pushing inside her, and then she'd be cleaning herself up.

He flashed her a wicked grin that was full of sensual promise, and she nearly fell off him from shock.

"I'll show ye." In one swift move, he had her on her back and was looming over her, his hair framing his face, and that wicked grin—the one she could kiss all day—returned to lips.

"Nay, not so quick," she whined, feeling completely comfortable in telling him that.

"Oh, it willna be quick, my *leannan troda*. Not quick at all."

Had he just called her his beloved fighter? Before she could wrap her head around the endearment, he pressed his lips to hers, that steely part of him rubbing tantalizingly against her slick sex, but rather than worry, she trusted.

Actually trusted.

The notion was completely foreign to her, and freeing at the same time. When he gripped her hands and put them over her head, deepening their kiss, she allowed it. She let herself fall into the kiss, not away from it. Unlike her other bed partners, when she tried to forget where she was and who she was with, Alesia was completely absorbed by Thor. Her Thornley.

She didn't want this moment to end. Ever.

Thor kissed his way along her jaw, enveloping her in pleasure and the masculine scent of him. She watched the way he moved over her. The way the muscles rippled from him holding up his weight on either side of her. When he whispered in her ear how beautiful she was, how he didn't think he could even be as happy as he was at that moment, she felt like she was soaring through the clouds, well above the sea.

All the worries of the past twenty years, her fears over the meeting with Santiago, melted away.

This was his doing. Their doing.

As much as she'd teased about coincidences, maybe there really was more to it than that. How was it possible that she could have met the one man who had the power to make her see life in a different way?

Her thoughts fell away as he kissed lower, laving at her breasts before trailing hot kisses over her belly. She sucked in her breath, falling deeper under the spell of pleasure. Thick hands spread over her thighs, urging her to let them fall open, and she complied, peeking through eyes she'd not known were closed to watch as he settled himself between her legs, his mouth inches from the dark curls that covered her sex. He winked at her and licked his lips like he was about to dine at the most exquisite of feasts.

Alesia knew what he was going to do. No man had ever done such to her, but she'd been around the wharf and brothels enough to know exactly what was about to happen. The women spoke of pleasure to die for.

And she wanted to die from it. Wanted to feel the smooth heat of his—

She didn't have to wait. Thor spread her folds with his fingers and flicked his tongue out over the tiny pink pearl that sent a shot of white-hot pleasure thundering through her.

"Oh my," she moaned, gripping the sheet on the mattress, and staring down at him.

His eyes locked on hers as he did it again, and she jolted. This was magic. Utter magic. Alesia watched him thrill her with his mouth until she could barely breathe, then she fell back on the bed, her back arched, eyes squeezing shut before popping them back open to watch. She didn't want to miss a single moment of this. She wanted to remember what he did, but the pleasure of it was so intense, it was difficult to comply with her own desire.

Pleasure won out. She writhed with his ministrations, shifting between clutching the mattress and his hair. He growled against her throbbing flesh as he quickened his pace. And she thought she must have died, sunk to the bottom of the sea and been captured by a god.

"Och, lass, ye taste so good."

"Dinna stop, please," she begged.

"I willna." And he didn't, even when her body broke apart into a thousand shards and his tongue completely obliterated her with pleasure.

She lay limp on the bed, her breaths sharp, face hot, legs shaking, and then he was hovering over her, a smile of pure male satisfaction on his face. "Permission to board, lass?" His smile turned teasing, and Alesia couldn't help but burst out laughing.

"Aye. Board me, pirate."

He slid up her body, kissing her with demanding force, her scent on his lips fascinating. And then she felt him probing.

"Have ye...are ye...?" He seemed to struggle with his question.

"I'm nay a virgin, Thornley. Please. Dinna make me wait."

With his forehead pressed to hers, he said, "Guide me in. I want this to be completely your choice."

Keeping her gaze locked on his, she did as he asked, her fingers wrapping around his solid, velvet length. He gritted his teeth and let out a groan.

"Will it end now?" she asked.

"Not if I can help it." There was such determination in his voice, such passion.

Alesia guided his thick member to the place where she wanted him to part her, consume her, own her.

Beads of sweat formed on his brow, and the muscles in his neck strained from the control he worked to maintain. The sight of that, besides sending another frisson of deep wanting to her core, also made her smile.

Eyes heavily lidded with passion met hers. "Tell me when, *leannan troda*."

"How long can ye wait?" Oh, she was wicked, teasing him like that.

His strong legs trembled, pressing to hers, the hair tickling the sensitive skin of her inner thighs.

"Forever."

"I canna, Thornley. Dinna make me wait that long."

"As ye wish."

She let go of his shaft, and he surged forward, filling her up. She waited for the inevitable pain of his invasion, but there was nothing beyond a sharp need, a hunger for more pleasure, that ultimate climax. Alesia grabbed hold of his muscular arms, clinging to him, wrapping her legs around his hips.

"*Mo chreach, leannan troda*. Am I still alive?" He pressed his forehead to hers and kissed her gently on the lips.

"More than alive, else I, too, am dead."

"Died and gone to heaven."

"Is that allowed for us?"

"Aye. Neither of us deserves the fires of hell."

"Let us not talk about the afterlife. Let us just enjoy this life."

"Och, aye, we'll enjoy the hell out of it."

Alesia giggled, slid her hand up around the back of his neck and tugged him down to kiss her. Kiss her he did, at the same time he started to move within her. Sliding out at a slow, delicious pace and then thrusting back inside, hitting a place deep within that sent showers of pleasure along her limbs.

"Move with me," he whispered against her ear.

"I dinna know how."

Thor gripped her hips, and as he withdrew, pushed her rear into the bed, but as he thrust forward, he tugged her up, so that her pelvis met his with a pulsing force. She moaned, quickly catching on to what he wanted her to do and moving with him.

His pace was slow and steady, then hard and fast, bringing her to the brink of that marvelous explosion and then pulling back. Torturing her, is what he was doing. Sweet, delicious, sensual torture. When she could take it no longer, she hooked her ankles at the small of his back, dug her nails into his shoulders and demanded he continue.

"I need...it. I want...it." She panted. "Dinna stop. I beg ye."

Thor growled something unintelligible, though she did pick up on one of the curses. Apparently, she was tormenting him just as much.

"God, I hope ye're close."

"Aye, so close. Dinna stop." She leaned up, tugged his lip between her teeth and plunged her tongue into his mouth, delighting in the way his kiss mirrored his arousal.

Acquiescing to her demands, he drove into her with abandon, their pelvises creating a delicious friction with each gyration, until a climax more powerful than the one she'd experienced before took hold, shoving her off that precipice. She rode the waves of pleasure, crying out his name, burying her face in his shoulder and soaking up the shuddering of his body.

"Blood and bones," he muttered against the side of her neck, sending her body into a riot of shivers. "That was...incredible."

"Ye were right." She nuzzled his shoulder, breathing in his scent, which was now combined with her own.

"About?" He traced a line along her face.

"Ye said ye'd make it last…and I…I had no idea it could be like this."

"Truth be told, neither did I." Thor rolled to the side, tugging her with him and stroking her hair down her spine.

Her hand lay over his still heavily beating heart, her leg over his warm thigh, and she thought nothing had ever felt so right than being in his arms.

"Give me a few minutes and we can do it again?" He winked, a devilish smile on his face.

A shiver of anticipation rushed through her. "Oh, aye. I'm not sure ye'll ever get me out of this cabin. Forget the crew. Forget Santiago. This bed is my whole new world." She giggled, and he tickled her naked ribs, leaning down to gently bite her on the hip, his beard tickling her skin. They wrestled for a few moments until they were both breathless with laughter.

"Lass, ye're a wee devil. Ye'll fit right in with the crew."

"A place I finally belong," she murmured.

The thrill of lying with him, the bliss, the subsequent calm, the feelings of trust were enough to make tears of joy come to her eyes, which also made her feel weak. And she'd just confessed, without thinking, that she felt like she belonged. Why had she allowed herself to get ahead of the situation? Nothing good had ever happened in her life. What made her think that this was any different?

CHAPTER FOURTEEN

*A*fter making love for the third time, Alesia fell sleep. Dark lashes fanned over flushed cheeks, and her wild raven hair spread out over the pillow in disarray. She looked thoroughly ravished. Gorgeous. Sensual. Thor kissed her gently on her slightly swollen lips. Having slept beside her for the previous three nights, Thor could tell this sleep was particularly deep. He'd worn her out. Hell, she'd worn him out, too.

He lay back against the pillows, one arm beneath her soft body and the other over his eyes. Edgard had seen that food was delivered to them at one point and everyone else had left them alone without question, but now he needed to get back out on deck. He needed to speak with his men about the upcoming battle they would no doubt engage in with Santiago.

While it had been a decadent, sensual foray into paradise, Thor could not remain abed forever, as much as he wanted to. He was captain of the vessel, and the principal leader of the other ships that followed. While Shaw and Con outranked him within the brethren, they had both decided this was Thor's mission, and he should head it.

Which meant he had a job to do.

Sailing the ship to the meeting point would be easy. It was afterward that was concerning. Without a doubt, he knew he could not allow Alesia to walk across a boarding plank onto Santiago's ship and out of his life. Not even if he planned to rescue her later. She had to stay on the *Leucosia* where she would be safe. Every man in the brethren would protect her with his life. That was the case the moment he'd brought her on board, but now that they knew she was his, their efforts would be doubled.

He needed to formulate a better plan than the one he had. One that would ensure a payout for the brethren but also ensure her safety.

How was he even going to tell Santiago about Alesia? The very thought of it turned his stomach. The Spanish captain was a bastard of the first order. If he had even an inkling of how Thor felt about Alesia, the man would no doubt, attempt to exploit it. Both he and Alesia were used to hiding their feelings, their reactions, but this was so new, so powerful, was it possible they would be as well put together as they normally were?

He couldn't risk it.

Ballocks! Thor cursed silently and gently removed himself from beneath the lass, tucking the covers around her body to keep her warm from the heat he'd taken away. She sighed and rolled to her side, as peaceful in her slumber as he was all tied up in knots.

He dressed quickly and then made his way out on deck. The sun was starting to set, showing pink on the horizon, and a gentle breeze blew off the sea. They'd made love all day. Discovering each other. Memorizing every line and curve. Every spot that tickled. Every touch that made the other gasp. Thor had never spent a day like that with a woman. Aye, he'd had plenty of bed partners in the past. Plenty of women he'd explored, but never any so intensely, and never had he allowed them the same pleasure at discovering him. This had been completely different. Mind altering, earth shattering. He felt like a new man upon the sun hitting his face.

With each passing minute he'd spent with Alesia, he'd fallen deeper.

Into what, he didn't want to contemplate. To know that he was *in deep* was enough to give him heart palpitations and make him question every decision he'd ever made, every decision he would consider in the future.

"Captain," Edgard said, yanking him from his thoughts.

What the hell was the matter with him? How could he have allowed her to distract him that intently?

"Edgard. What is our status?" Thor forced his thoughts from his head—a physical struggle to be sure—and focused on the sea beyond and his crew.

"We're set to reach the coordinates on time, Captain."

"Any issues along the way?"

"None."

Thor nodded, approaching the helm and checking his compass. The air was chilly, crisp, and though there were a few wispy clouds in the sky, he felt confident they'd not be impeded by weather. They sailed at a steady clip, and the waters were smooth.

Trailing behind them were *The Sea Devil, Savage of the Sea* and *The Gaia*. Four ships against Santiago's small armada were good odds. Even if the bastard traveled with half a dozen ships, the brethren would be more than fine going up against him. The Pirates of Britannia had state-of-the-art weaponry, their canons newer, their armor more dangerous. Not to mention that Thor was sailing the precious *Leucosia*.

The ship had previously belonged to Santiago. At the time she was stolen by Santiago from the Dutch, she had been called the *Astorga*. She was a beauty with her twenty-two guns. Con had rammed the side of the ship several months ago, boarded her and taken control. Santiago had been furious at Con for taking his prized ship, and had been after him to get her back ever since.

Of course, to confuse the Spaniard, Con had passed the *Leucosia* off to Shaw in one of their endless battles to outwit each other. But even after refitting the spectacular galley to her current condition, including the newly painted ship's name, Shaw, had known the difference and marked her as the *Astorga*. Which, Thor had found out, was why they had tussled in the tavern.

No matter. The point was, Santiago would know she was his ship and would want her back. Badly.

Con thought that since he'd spared Santiago's captain, a man nicknamed Little Devil, in the attack on the *Astorga*, he would be merciful now to the brethren, honoring a code of mercy, but Thor knew better. He'd seen the bastard and his merciless heart firsthand. Had the scars to prove it.

He touched his face, tracing the long line down his cheek. That had been courtesy of Santiago when he'd captured him several years back. A jagged, curved dagger.

Bloody bones of the devil. What the hell was he thinking putting Alesia in this position?

And what made Thor think she wouldn't choose her blood over him? What made him think that though he had fallen for her and she'd enjoyed a day of passion with him, that he meant enough to her that she'd forgo the man bound to by blood.

The lass had admitted to not having a family, how she longed to belong. How she felt that she belonged with the brethren, with Thor. But Santiago was most certainly her father. There was no doubt in anyone's mind. She was a hell of a lot prettier than the sorry maggot, but their coloring and temper were the same. Once she caught sight of him, wouldn't she feel the pull of blood ties to cross over to the Spanish ship?

"Everything all right, Cap'n?" Edgard stood beside him, looking quite concerned.

"Aye." Thor turned his attention back to the sea. The sooner they got through with this the better. If only she had been a lad he could have simply tossed into his ship's dungeon. That would have made all of this so much easier.

But she had to be her. And he had to fall in love with her.

Aye, that's what had happened. That burning in his chest, the emotional swells and tugs was love. He'd figured it out. The sentiment was intense, and he was disgusted at himself for allowing her to wiggle her way into his heart. Hadn't he vowed not to love another after having lost all he'd loved as a lad? Hadn't he vowed his entire existence was to get his revenge on Santiago? Love didn't play into that. A woman didn't have a place within his life. And yet, in the span of a sennight, he'd essentially made Alesia the center of his world.

"Take the helm," he growled.

He had to settle this. Face it head on. He marched to the cabin, banged the door open and startled the lass from her sleep. She bolted upright in bed, but upon seeing him, she smiled languidly. Dark tendrils of wild hair covered half her face, and she gave an indolent yawn and stretched her arms over her head.

"Ye scared me," she admitted, her lips curled in a sensual smile.

Thor slammed the door closed and backed against it, crossing his arms over his chest as if standing like that would make his heart stay in place. Her smile fell.

"This time tomorrow, the battle will be over." Every word

was like a knife scraping over his throat. "Ye'll either be dead, or I'll be dead."

"What?" Alesia ran her hands through her hair, trying to work through what he was saying and settling her narrowed eyes on him.

"I'm going to get ye killed, Miss Baird. Or ye're going to get me killed."

The change in her was instant. The hardness that came into her eyes made his heart clench with regret. "I dinna see how that is possible, *Captain* Thor."

Thor cursed under his breath. Not only had she picked up on his formal use of her name, she was tossing it back at him. Banging the heel of his boot hard against the door, he let it all out in a rush before he could pull it back. "I love ye, lass. And I willna be able to hide that fact. Which means Santiago will kill me for loving ye, or kill ye to get back at me."

The lass's eyes widened to the size of the rising sun, her mouth forming a similar sized O. "Why should he go to such extremes?"

"Because he—" Thor cut himself off. Aye, he'd already told her his name, something he'd never told anyone else. This was something closer to the heart than his name. He'd told her that Santiago ruined his life, but he never shared the whole story. Fists balled at his sides, Thor stood there frozen, uncertain how to tell her. Uncertain how to even come to grips with the emotions pummeling his insides like the mudslides or avalanches in his Highland home.

Alesia gracefully stood from the bed, wrapped a plaid about her body and walked determinedly toward him. There was no censure in her face. No judgment. No pity in her gaze, which he wouldn't have been able to stand. Only concern. It was the exact opposite of what he wanted her to show, and irritatingly, just what he needed. When he looked at her, he knew the truth. He loved her. Loved her hard. And there was no escaping that. If only she could have judged him, hated him, it would make turning away from her all the easier.

She came to stop a foot or so in front of him. Enough to be close, but not to crowd, waiting for him to invite her the rest of the way into his space. Thor ground his teeth, stared into her eyes and saw his own emotions reflected there. Was it possible that she…loved him, too?

"What happened?" she inquired softly, reaching for his arm and sliding a finger over where he'd crossed them until he let them fall apart. "What has the power to break down the mighty Thor?"

Her words, spoken partially in jest, were stronger than their humor reflected. And spot on. What did have the power to take him down?

Thor reached for her hand, tugging her slim fingers into his grasp. He rubbed his thumb along the knuckles, seeking to absorb some of the strength she seemed to have a boundless stock of.

"He took something from me." He kept his gaze on their joined hands, unable to look her in the eyes, afraid that if he did, his tongue would dry up and the words wouldn't come.

She waited patiently, but after a dozen heartbeats, she urged, "What?"

Thor took a deep steadying breath, and finally looked her in the eye. "My mother."

Alesia's eyes widened a fraction of an inch as she met his gaze. "Prisoner?"

But he could see the truth of what she knew in her gaze. "Nay."

No longer waiting for his invitation, she tucked herself against him. Her wild hair tickled his neck, as her hands splayed on his back. "I'm so sorry. Ye dinna have to tell me if ye dinna want to."

The words tumbled out in a stream of consciousness as he relived those moments, unable to stop himself.

"My father was a Viking. He married my mother, daughter of the MacLeod chief, in an effort to solidify an alliance. But he never meant to keep the alliance. He allied with Santiago, invited the bastard into our home to rob them of everything. But my mother, she was a warrior. And she hated my father. He'd never been kind to her. He'd gotten her with child—with me—and abandoned us all until that day he returned with Santiago Fernandez. It was near Yule. I remember the snow falling clearly, big snowflakes that danced against the torchlights like magic. The ships came. The men falling from the vessels like a horde of ants into our castle. Our warriors fought, but they lost, and when Santiago entered the great hall with my father, the look of betrayal on my mother's face is one I'll never forget."

"Oh, Thornley." Alesia squeezed him tighter and pressed her lips to his heart.

Still, he couldn't stop retelling it. "I was hiding in an alcove, the laird's lug, and I heard and saw it all. My father stood by while Santiago killed my mother. And then the bastard killed my father, too. He wanted all the treasure for himself." He drew in an unsteady breath. "I've been hunting him my entire life. 'Tis how he captured me afore. I managed to escape, which bruised his ego. He's a cruel devil, parading himself as a merchant pirate. And I know the truth. And I know it will end with one of our deaths."

"It doesna have to be that way." She was gazing up at him now, tears wetting her eyes.

"I see no other way." Thor hardened his jaw, determined to see an end to this struggle today.

Alesia shook her head. "Because ye're too blinded by your pain."

He glared down at her, angry and unwilling to admit she might speak the truth.

"What do ye know of my pain? Your mother was—"

"Dinna say it, Thor." Her grip on him loosened. "Dinna say something ye canna take back. I know more than anyone who and what my mother was. Though ye lost your mother, at least ye can look back with fond memories. I will never be able to do that."

Instantly, he felt like an arse for the bitter words he'd been about to utter. He didn't even mean them. Alesia didn't deserve his ire. There was only one man who did—Santiago.

"I'm sorry, lass." He pressed his forehead to hers. "I shouldna have even thought it."

Her eyelids dipped down. "Anger makes us lash out and say things we dinna mean."

"I should be able to control that."

She smiled, reached up and stroked his cheek, then gave a little tug on his beard, a habit she'd picked up that he found endearing. "Sometimes our emotions get in the way of being able to control our mouths."

"Or fists." He raised a questioning brow.

"Aye, ye're verra lucky I didna try to fight ye just now."

He chuckled and tucked her back against him, pressing his lips to the top of her head. "I have to tell ye something."

She tried to look up at him, but he kept her head firmly tucked to his chest, fearing that if he were to look into her eyes, he'd not be able to confess what needed confessing. This time, she didn't urge him to speak. She simply waited.

"I love ye, Alesia Baird."

"What?" Her tone was that of surprise, but because he couldn't see her face, he couldn't gauge her reaction. A mistake, because he realized then and there he needed so very badly to see if she might return his affections.

Thor tipped her chin, looked her in the eye and said, "I

love ye with every part of my being. I dinna know when it started. 'Haps when I saw ye on the docks. But I do. Every part of ye. From your bristly tongue to your fighting fists to your constantly bare feet. When I'm not with ye, I think about ye. When I'm with ye, I canna stop thinking about how to make ye smile. And knowing that on the morrow we will face my enemy, and I will have brought ye into harm's way, I hate myself."

"Oh, Thornley…" She gripped his shirt tightly, pulling the fabric taut against his back.

He feared seeing what he'd done in her eyes. He was ashamed. "I'll never forgive myself."

She tugged at his beard. "Look at me."

Though his stomach was tied up in knots, he did as she asked, looking deep into her green eyes and seeing nothing that he feared there.

"Dinna hate yourself. Dinna berate yourself. I brought myself into this mess, not ye."

"Not if I hadna put out the call for Santiago's bairn."

"But do ye not see?" She smiled softly. "If ye hadna, we'd never have met. We'd not have found each other. We'd not have fallen in love."

Blood and bones, he felt as vulnerable as he had when he was a wee lad watching his mother die. Everything was hanging in the balance. His life. His future. His love. And she'd said… "We… ye said *we*."

"Aye." A radiant smile broke out on her lips. "I love ye, too, my Thornley. And there is no one I would rather go to battle with. No one I would rather fight beside. No one I would rather trust, love, cherish. I've been searching my whole life to belong. To matter and have a purpose, and with ye, I have found it."

A joy he'd never known encircled its way around his steel heart, warming him, melting him entirely.

"I will turn this ship around right now," he vowed.

"Nay, ye willna. Because loving me doesna mean ye have to give up on your revenge." She winked and playfully tapped her fist against his heart.

He chuckled. "Ye're a bloodthirsty wench."

"Perhaps." She leaned up on her tiptoes and brushed her mouth over his. "If he is my sire, as ye suspect, then I want to be there when he falls."

"I am half tempted to thank him for being your father."

She playfully slapped at him again. "Only if your sword is running through his heart at the same time."

Thor lifted her up and twirled her around. "A lass after my own heart."

CHAPTER FIFTEEN

*A*lesia leaned up for Thor's kiss when the door behind him rattled.

"Cap'n! Come quick! We've spotted sails at our stern."

"Bloody hell." Thor kissed her hard and fast and then was through the door before Alesia could truly process what was happening. All the warmth and security she'd felt in the moments they'd shared evaporated and were replaced by thick clouds of panic in her chest.

Sails. Ship's sails. Coming from the opposite direction of where they were headed. Why would he be worried, unless the sails were those of an enemy…

Oh God… She clutched at her chest, knees buckling. Before she could fall to the floor in horror, Alesia shut the door firmly and hurried to dress. Breeches, shirt, roped belt and boots. She hopped from one foot to the other, blinded herself with her shirt over her eyes in an effort to hurry through the process. She nearly tripped over a chair, bashed her knee on the bed and hit her head on the wall. No time to brush or plait her hair, she swept it up in an attempt at a knot and tied it off with ribbon and then burst from the cabin.

She hurried along the galley toward the ladder that led up to the main deck, but she could not hear her footsteps above the noise that sounded overhead and below. Men ran and shouted. Beneath her feet, the wood planks vibrated as the cannons were rolled into place and possibly even loaded in the level below.

On deck, the sun shone bright, partially blinding her as her eyes adjusted. Holding a hand up to shield its blinding power, she searched out the helm where a crewman manned the massive wheel. Not Thor. Not Edgard, either.

Alesia walked steadily forward, turning in a circle and examining every man and swab. None of them as large as Thor. Where was he?

A whistle sounded above, and she glanced up, shielding her eyes to see that he stood on a platform attached to the main mast dozens of feet in the air. What had she heard that called before? Oh, aye, the crow's nest. His black shirt billowed in the wind, and because he wore a plaid…it was also billowing. She quickly looked away before anyone noticed that she'd just spotted his… Well, that she'd seen the plaid flapping in the wind.

He was signaling to the other ships in their party and pointing out a few white specs on the horizon. Those must be the sails. Without any discernable markings, it was hard to ascertain just who it was. Royal Navy ships, merchants, pirates, enemies. It could be anyone.

Alesia ran toward the stern to get a better view, leaping over swabs at work and the rigging on the deck. An over-turned crate had spilled straw and chickens that were now squawking and rushing about the ship as though they'd only just realized they were not safely tucked away at a farm. She couldn't help but think she kind of felt like the chickens. Panicked and scared.

Uncertain.

The swabs adjusted their sails, as did the men on the other ships, gaining speed and moving away from their pursuers. For a little while, it appeared they were in fact gaining, the white sails in the distance creeping out of view, but then she realized it was only the way the sun had blocked them. Though they were not any closer, they were not any further away.

"I need a weapon," she muttered, realizing that her fists would not help her if they were boarded by men with swords and pistols.

Alesia had fired a pistol before, in a tavern when she'd been mayhap ten or eleven summers. Two men were fighting over one of the whores she'd called Aunt Agatha. The woman wasn't a relation, or at least not that she'd known of. But for a short time after her mother died, Aunt Agatha had been willing to feed her. But to earn her keep, Alesia had to steal from the woman's customers. In any case, when one of the men figured out their scheme, he went after Aunt Agatha with a murderous fury. Another of Agatha's customers hadn't wanted to see her shot, and so the two men had battled it out. When the would-be rescuer had fallen dead and the attacker held his gun at Aunt Agatha's head, Alesia had done the only thing she could think of. She'd picked up the discarded weapon and fired. First time firing a weapon, and she'd hit her mark head on—literally. There'd been a smoky hole with a trickle of blood centered in the middle of his forehead. She was a natural shot with good aim. Perhaps from having to judge spaces to disappear into or steal from. She'd never really thought of it, only that she could.

And she needed a pistol right now. Or at the very least, a crossbow.

Alesia whirled from the bow of the ship and searched the deck. The chickens were still running amuck while the swabs tried to catch them. Even as fast as they were going, the enemy ships were still gaining on them. She could hear Thor overhead shouting orders to his men, and the orders of the captains from the other brethren ships echoed on the wind.

Then she saw a shiny pistol set behind one of the spilled crates, perhaps dropped by one of the lads as they chased a chicken. She surged forward and lifted it up. Was it loaded? Was there any way to tell?

Realizing that if it was loaded, she'd only get off one shot and then be helpless since she didn't know how to reload, and if it wasn't loaded, she'd be equally in trouble because it would be pointless as a weapon. Alesia set the pistol back down and again whirled in the chaos on deck.

"Miss Baird, ye must get back to your cabin."

She spun to face Edgard. "What?" There was no doubting the incredulousness in her tone, and the man took a step back, perhaps wondering if she was going to raise her fists to him or use the discarded pistol.

Alesia took a deep breath, realizing he had every right to worry. She was so used to raising her fists, to fighting for what she wanted, or what she thought she deserved, it was as automatic to her as breathing. Stepping back from him, she forced her fingers to unfurl, to press her palms to her thighs.

"I'm not going back to the cabin, Edgard. I can help. I want to help."

The first mate *tsked*. "Lass, ye must. The cap'n's orders."

Alesia shot a glance up to the mast to where she'd last seen Thor, but he was no longer in the perch.

"Where is he?"

Edgard didn't have to ask whom she meant. There was only one man she sought. "Gone bellow to check on the guns, miss. Asked me to make sure ye were safely in the cabin."

"I want to speak to him. I'm certain he'll change his

mind." Squaring her shoulders, she put on her best authoritative face. "Take me to him."

Edgard shook his head. "Nay, lass, I canna."

"Then I shall find him myself." She started to move around Edgard when his fingers gripped her elbow before quickly dropping.

The move was enough to make her halt—but only for a second. Alesia stared down at his grip on her, actually seeing the moment he changed his mind and his fingertips went from white to pink. She lifted her chin and started to march toward the middle of the ship where she'd seen many of the swabs climbing down a ladder. The ship's cannons had to be located down there. And if not, she'd ask—nay, demand someone point her in the right direction.

Again, she felt Edgard's fingers grip her arm, only this time he did not let go. The poor man looked like he was going to be sick.

"Apologies, Miss Baird, but the cap'n said if I let ye get away from me it would be my head, and whilst I think ye're a pretty lass, I do quite like my head where it is. So if ye wouldna give me so much trouble, I'll just be taking ye back to your cabin." There was a slight tremble to his fingers, though he held her fast. He was staring at her expectantly, begging almost.

She had half a mind to give him what he expected—a good fight—except that would only cause a scene and get her well and truly locked up. Perhaps going back to the cabin was the best course of action, as Thor likely had a weapon stashed there that she could use.

All pirates had multiple weapons, and what better place than in the room he slept and prepared for his day.

Of course, thinking of where he slept brought about the image of the bed, and what he'd done with her there. Her cheeks flushed pink, and she glanced away from Edgard's intense gaze, afraid he'd be able to see right into her head and know just what wicked things she'd been thinking of. And at a time like this… Oh, she was wicked. Well, she knew that already. Thor just seemed to bring out the worst and best in her.

"All right," she grumbled, "but ye needna hold on to me like I'm a criminal. I'm no more wanted for the gibbet than the rest of ye scoundrels."

"If I let go—"

She cut him off before he could go on. "I will not run away. In fact, ye can watch me go if ye want."

"I'll need to see ye shut in, if ye dinna mind, lass." He tapped his head. "On account of the cap'n's warning."

She held the urge to roll her eyes and nodded instead. "Then let me at least take your elbow, and we can stroll about the ship as if nothing is happening and we are just two people going for a walk."

"What?" He screwed up his face in confusion, and Alesia held back her laughter.

"Oh, come now, Edgard, as handsome as ye are, ye canna tell me that ye havena walked about town with a lass on your arm?"

Now it was his turn to blush.

Oh, aye, Alesia was certainly a ruffian by any lady's standards, but she knew how to stroke the ego of any man or woman to get what she wanted—even if that meant pretending to be something she wasn't.

Not allowing him time to continue sputtering in case they caught the attention of anyone on board, she grabbed his elbow and started to drag him down the main deck toward the stairs that led down to the captain's quarters. It didn't take him long to catch up to her, and she ignored his look of surprise as she walked into the cabin, smiled at him and shut the door in his face.

She waited behind the closed doors until she heard his footsteps fade away, afraid Thor might have also been given orders to lock her in.

Thankfully, he did not lock the door.

Breathing a sigh of relief, she whirled about to face the room, for there was no time to waste. The cabin was set up very similarly to the one on *The Sea Devil*, and for a moment, she panicked that perhaps Thor had not brought all of his own weaponry on board. She first dug through a massive chest, picking the secret lock hidden on top instead of bothering with the dummy lock on the front. She knew how these things worked. She never would have survived as long as she had if she didn't.

Inside the chest was a stash of rum, some blankets and a beautiful sword scabbard. She thought that it would be a good weapon to use, except when she opened it, she found the blade to be so tiny, one would barely even use it for an eating knife.

"Useless," she muttered. Was that some sort of joke? If she didn't know better, she'd say that Thor had already been here and planted that ridiculous excuse for a weapon to taunt her.

The chest contained nothing much else of use, so she shut it back up and moved to the bed. As she suspected, after tugging the mattress from the frame, there was a secret compartment, and while it had some precious metals and jewels inside that she would very much like to take, they wouldn't help in saving her arse if she ended up at the end of some scoundrel's blade or pistol.

Not bothering to put the mattress back, she marched over to the desk on the far wall and searched through the drawers, finding a seal breaker, a flint and a few scraps of parchment. Nothing, absolutely nothing. Much the same as the desk on board *The Sea Devil*. What was with these boring pirates?

This was not the plan at all, and she found herself

growing quite frustrated. So frustrated, she slammed her hand against the wall, feeling the sudden burst that usually came from fighting.

But also sudden shock.

For the wall panels swung open to reveal an arsenal. Holy pirates, she'd never seen so many weapons in one place. Swords, daggers, pistols, long guns, crossbows, maces, axes and a few things she wasn't quite sure of. She had her pick of weapons.

A squeal of excitement bubbled from her throat.

There was no way she wasn't going to be in this fight now. Thor could just try and stop her.

CHAPTER SIXTEEN

*N*o matter what tactic he tried, Thor couldn't shake their pursuers. By now, he was convinced it was Santiago's armada in pursuit. He wasn't surprised. The man had been the one to set the meeting place. In fact, when Mari had given the coordinates to Lachlan to relay to Thor, she'd done so with a warning that nothing was as it seemed, and not to underestimate their enemy. Apparently, Santiago had had a spark in his eye that Mari had found suspicious.

Likely, Santiago had planned an ambush all along.

So to see the sails that pursued them was expected. And now that Thor was certain of the identity of their pursuer, he was confident and ready to put the plan he'd made with Shaw, Con, Kelly and Lachlan into place.

Giving the pre-planned signal to the other ships, Thor went below to make sure the lads were loading up the cannons. Thor ran his hand over the smooth and polished cool iron. They were much the same as his own aboard *The Sea Devil*, though these were shinier, never fired. The lads stood proudly beside their weapons, thrilled with the idea of lighting the fuse.

"Are they loaded?" Thor asked.

"Aye, Cap'n. Loaded with the iron cannonballs ye had commissioned."

Special cannonballs. Before he'd boarded the *Leucosia*, he'd had his men switch out the ammunition on *The Sea Devil*, to this ship. They were each etched with the words, *Feel the wrath of Thor*. He'd chuckled at the time, having commissioned them after losing a bet to Con. He'd yet to have the pleasure of using them, because when most pirates saw the Devils of the Deep sails, they surrendered almost immediately.

But now, the very idea of having these custom iron balls of wrath hurtling through the air and puncturing the hull of Santiago's ships made Thor smile with satisfaction.

"Good. Be prepared to fire on my signal."

"Aye, Cap'n."

Thor nodded to the lads and promised them that the battle they were about to embark on would line their pockets with gold. And he meant to see that it did, no matter the outcome. He slid down the ladders into the bowels of the ship, wishing the rowers well and promising extra meat with their supper and a week's worth of boozing and wenching when their mission was complete. That sent up a deafening cheer.

Once more on deck, Thor signaled to Edgard to swing the helm, turning the rudders about. They were going to meet Santiago head on. Finally, after all these times. After so many moments when Thor thought he was close, but Santiago always seemed to disappear into thin air.

A hum of excitement whirled in his blood, and he couldn't help but grin as he marched toward the bow of the ship and watched her make the one hundred eighty degree turn until she faced Santiago's armada. As he'd guessed, they outnumbered the ships by one. Ironic, given their one extra ship was Santiago's.

With a crude gesture in his enemy's direction, Thor made his way back to the helm.

"Look alive, lads! Today is the day we face down our enemies and watch their blood stain the water. The Devils of the Deep will reign supreme!"

"Ho-aye!" the men shouted before starting up an old pirate song about battles and blood and victory.

Thor couldn't help the satisfied grin on his face. He flexed his fingers and cracked his neck. The past two decades were finally coming to a head. All that he'd worked for. All he'd ever wanted. Santiago's head in his hands. To feel the warmth of the bastard's blood slipping through his fingers. An image of Alesia flashed before his mind, and with it instant guilt.

But why should he feel guilty? This was everything he'd worked for. The reason he'd agreed to join the brethren instead of running away. He could have very well become a wharf rat like her. He could have refused his post as captain. At any point over the last twenty years, he could have left the pirates and gone rogue, possibly even infiltrated the Spanish, though it would have been hard to disguise himself given his size.

He gazed around at the men on the ship, then over toward the *Savage of the Sea* where Shaw, his prince of pirates, saluted him as he scaled the mast toward the crow's nest.

There was no going back. And if he'd ever had any doubts, the feeling of gratitude and pride he got from saluting Shaw back was telling enough. This was where he belonged. These men were his family, and it was time to eradicate the threat. Alesia would understand. She had to. She'd said as much herself. She didn't even know if Santiago was her father, and if he was… Och, if he was, then she had every right to thrust a blade through his chest for the torments she'd been made to suffer all of her life.

Thor muttered an oath. The sea that stretched out from the *Leucosia* to their enemies was closing swiftly. Thor battled between the urges to collect Alesia so she could fight beside him, or to order her locked in the cabin for her own safety. But if there was one thing he'd learned about the lass, it was that if he locked her in, she'd only escape. She was a fighter, and if she wanted in on this battle, there would be no stopping her.

The revelation made him smile with pride. They were meant to be together, no two were a more perfect pair.

If he couldn't stop her, he should invite her to join him.

With that resolution in mind, he turned from the helm, prepared to march to the cabin and ask her if she would like to join him, to arm her with weapons. To kiss her before they raised their swords.

But upon turning around, what he saw stopped him cold. Standing before him was Alesia dressed in breeches, the sleeves of her shirt rolled up to the elbows revealing leather-studded bracers on her forearms. She had on an armored vest studded with iron. In one hand, she had a crossbow, and there was a targe strapped to the forearm of her opposite arm. A targe was a tiny shield on him, but looked normal on her. Draped over her shoulder was a quiver full of arrows for the crossbow, and crisscrossing her back were two swords. A leather belt was slung over her hips with a pistol on each side and two tiny daggers.

Whatever he'd been imagining her doing in the cabin at that moment had not been this. Och, but she never ceased to surprise him. What else would she have been doing in there besides arming herself? Certainly she wouldn't have been curled up in the corner or brushing out her hair. Nay, not his lass.

Alesia was a warrior woman bent on a good fight. Bent on destruction.

She was every man's nightmare.

Every man but him.

In fact, looking at her like this had Thor's heart melting the rest of the way, and a rush of desire flooding him.

Peering down, he fully expected to see her feet bare, but surprisingly, she'd strapped on her boots.

"Ye're beautiful," he said, without thinking. "And ye've got on boots."

"Fighting barefoot seemed too dangerous. 'Tis not too much?" She raised a brow, a hint of a smile on her luscious lips.

"Not by half." Thor strode across the deck, closing the distance between them. He reached for her, snaking an arm around her waist, avoiding the blades crossing at her back, and hauled her up against him. "Ye're a dream come true."

Not giving her a chance to reply, he bent his lips to hers and kissed her with all the passion he felt. Consuming, mind-altering, heart stopping. If he were to believe in such things as fate or soul mates, he would believe she was fated for him. He knew without a doubt she was meant for him. They had so much in common, he felt she knew him better than anyone else in the world. That if he were to part from her at this very moment, life would cease to matter.

"I love ye," he murmured against her lips. "I want ye to be mine."

She clutched the front of his shirt, dewy eyes gazing up at his, flames smoldering behind their green depths. "Yours?"

"No other man's. And I would belong to ye."

Her face flushed, and she tipped her head, eyes closing.

"Ye're an adventurer, Thor. I love ye too much to hold ye back."

"Ye dinna understand." He touched two fingers to her chin, forcing her to look up at him. "I want nothing else. I want to face the open seas with ye at my side. My life will be incomplete without ye. I mean it, Alesia. I want ye to be my wife."

Her mouth opened and closed, then opened again, but the only thing that came out was a long whoosh of air.

A pain gripped his chest, as though someone had reached inside and squeezed hard. Would she deny him after he'd bared his soul to her? Thor blew out a breath. "Ye dinna have to tell me now. We can fight this battle and then talk more about it, but we will talk."

She pressed her hands to his heart. "I would be honored to be your wife. But…"

Thor could guess the things she was about say. There was so much that came with being a wife—mainly all the things he couldn't see her being. She was never going to obey him, labor for him. She was a free spirit, had lived on her own for so long that she would never want to be ruled by anyone. And that was what he loved about her—her independent, free spirit. "I'll not take away your freedoms, lass. I just want ye by my side. Right beside me. Not behind me."

"Like Jane and Gregg." Her eyes were locked on his, brimming with hope but also apprehension. Her throat bobbed.

There was no hesitation in his answer. "Aye. Like Jane and Gregg."

A soft smile touched her lips, and she clutched his shirt tighter. "I want that, too."

"Then 'tis settled. When we beat him"—he jerked his head toward the oncoming ships—"and we will…we shall marry."

"What about before, when ye said we could not both live…that…" Her lip started to tremble, and she clenched her mouth closed for a moment. "That one or both of us would surely die today."

"I was a fool, Alesia, *leannan troda*." He cupped her face with his hands, feeling the warmth of her soft skin seep into his palms. "I could never let anything happen to ye, and I want to spend the rest of our lives wreaking havoc on the seas. How could I let that, let us, slip away?"

"Oh, ye do know how to speak to a woman's heart." Alesia leaned up on tiptoe, and he met her halfway, his mouth covering hers in a possessive, passion-filled kiss.

"Cap'n," Edgard called from the helm, interrupting their private, yet public, moment. "Your orders."

Reluctantly, Thor pulled his mouth from Alesia's, stared into her brilliant eyes and whispered, "I love ye."

"I love ye, too."

With one last quick kiss, he turned to his men.

"All hands, ahoy!" Thor took Alesia by the hand and went to the center of the deck to address his men. "Ready your sea legs, lads. The moment we've been waiting for is upon us. Behold, the Spanish bastards! There'll be no parley this day. We'll give no quarter. Today, we're going to blow the man down and take him for all he's worth."

A shout of agreement, a pirate's battle cry, went up among the crew. Alesia, too, joined in their cheers.

"Let them try to take what is ours. We shall show them what it means to fight the brethren. We are the Devils of the Deep, and together with Poseidon's Legion, *we* rule the seas."

"Aye-aye!"

"Get ye to your stations. Prepare for battle!" The men let out another booming cheer and then rushed to their duties. Power and battle lust coursed through Thor's veins. God, he'd been waiting so long for this moment. And to share it with the one he loved? Nothing could have made it better. "Are ye ready, lass?"

"Aye."

"Need a nip of *uisge beatha?*" He raised a brow.

"Nay. I never imbibe before a fight. But after, och, I will definitely need it then." She grinned, not a hint of fear in her eyes.

Blood and bones, he loved her confidence.

They stood at the helm, waiting as the ship barreled toward an uncertain fate, and all that mattered was that they were in this together.

CHAPTER SEVENTEEN

hough she'd managed to keep her trembling at bay, Alesia's heart could not cease its staccato beat. This was really happening. When she'd walked up on deck, seen the organized chaos of the men preparing for war, she'd been certain Thor would send her back to their cabin. That he would berate her for taking nearly everything she could find on that secret weapon wall. That he'd tell her war was no place for a woman. That he would deny her very existence and the thing that had kept her alive all these years— her ability to hold her own.

But the look he'd given her had been anything but anger. Anything but censure. His countenance had been…moving. It had made her chest thump with excitement. No one had ever looked at her like that. A mixture of astonishment, pride, love, desire. It was an expression she wanted him to give her over and over again for the rest of her life. Even if that happened to only be this day.

His big, warm hand engulfed hers, making her feel safe and secure. From where she stood with him at the bow, the

Spanish flags had come into view, and she could see the tiny dots of men moving about the ship. There was one at the bow—standing atop it and hanging on to the rigging.

Edgard was shouting again, preparing the Devils of the Deep for their meeting head on.

"Who will turn first?" she murmured.

"Not I. We never turn first," Thor murmured to her and then shouted to his crew, "Stand your ground! Stay the course!"

"Ye would rather hit them?" The men on the Spanish ships looked just as determined. The one hanging on the front didn't waver in the slightest.

"We willna." Thor was so confident, so sure. She tried to leech some of it from him, but she still found her belly doing too many flips for comfort.

"Why?" she asked, squeezing his hand tighter.

"Because"—he smiled down at her, his eyes steady, his brow smooth—"Santiago's already lost one ship to us, this verra one in fact. He won't want to lose another. Also"—he wiggled his brows with enthusiasm—"he knows I will not turn."

As Thor predicted, the man hanging off the front shouted something that didn't carry on the wind, and their ship abruptly slowed and turned. However, it did not to go around them. In fact, it turned so its starboard side faced them—along with their cannons, shining from the hull like black, vacant eyes. Even with the seventeen canons that she counted facing them, Thor did not seem concerned, so she tried not to be either—but it was harder to accomplish than she hoped.

Alesia studied the men onboard the ship, not recognizing any of them. They looked like pirates, to be sure, just like Thor's crew, only with olive-toned skin, dark, glossy hair and pointed beards. They all wore breeches and shirts of gold and crimson. They all appeared to be miniature versions of their captain, who was easy to see with his flamboyant hat and an ornately embroidered brocade vest in the same colors of gold and blood. The two ships with him also turned to their sides, pointing their guns at the brethren.

"Ho there!" Shaw's voice was heard over the wind as he called out to the Spaniards. "This is not the meeting point."

A bitter laugh sounded, coming from the direction of the galleys in front of them.

"And you are not Thor." Santiago turned his gaze from Shaw to the *Leucosia*. "That is my ship. No matter how many times a snake sheds his skin, he is still *una serpiente*."

A rumbled growl came from Thor's throat, and he stood taller, letting go of her hand to leap upon the rail like Santiago. "Och, no one tried to disguise the fact, but the snake reference… Are ye referring to yourself?"

Alesia listened quietly to the exchanges, fear gnawing at the calm reserve she hoped to convey.

"Did you bring what I asked for, *bastardo*?" Santiago shouted.

"Aye." Thor held out his hand to Alesia, urging her to take hold. For half a breath, she contemplated and then decided to continue taking the leaps she'd been hurtling ever since Thor first crossed her path. She grabbed hold of his hand and leapt up onto the rail, steadying herself beside him. "Ye'll have to come and get her yourself—with the bounty ye owe me."

"Her?" The man's voice was amused, but his brow furrowed, and behind his dark, long beard, his mouth turned down in what could only be discerned as disappointment.

Alesia tried not to be offended that he seemed somewhat put off that she was not a lad. For who was he to her? He was a stranger. A nobody. And even if he was her sire, he was no man she could ever respect for having left her mother and her to suffer, for having killed Thor's mother.

"Aye." This time it was Alesia that spoke. Unafraid now as she faced the man who could be her father.

Thor squeezed her hand and then nodded to his men. The rumble beneath her feet sounded as the men pushed the cannons forward to point at Santiago's ship.

"Perhaps the deal is *terminado*," Santiago called. "I was looking for a son."

"Ye're honor bound to see this deal through," Thor shouted, this time she did feel him trembling beside her, but with rage and indignation, never fear.

Aye, he was a pirate. Aye he wanted revenge, but he would not board Santiago's ship without reason. Was he hoping Santiago would give him that reason now?

"Honor bound?" she whispered, seeking clarification.

"Our brethren's code." Thor cursed. "Would that I could break it, but I canna."

He let go of her hand to rest his on his pistol, his jaw muscle ticking furiously.

"How will *la niña* prove she's mine?" Santiago's ship floated closer, and for the first time, Alesia could see just why the men of the Devils of the Deep did not question her parentage.

The man had the same glossy black hair as her, the same vibrant eyes. He seemed to take notice of it at the same time, a flash of pride coming over his face.

Bloody hell… She knew at that moment she could not kill him, whether he'd left her to starve or not. He might be a bastard, but she wasn't a murderer.

"Tell me the name of your *madre*." He swept his fingers down the length of his beard.

Alesia sucked in a breath and straightened her shoulders. "Scarlet Baird."

The wind whipped, causing her carefully pulled back hair to lash against her face, as though her mother were coming back from the dead to haunt her. Then the air seemed to suddenly still. Even the water no longer rippled, looking blank and black on the surface like a dark mirror of misery. The ships were reflected in the surface, and a few lines her mother sang to her on her deathbed finally made sense. *Our anchor's weighed, our sails are set. The friends we leave we'll never forget. Unless her name is poor Scarlet.*

Suddenly, all she felt for her mother was pity. All the animosity and resentment melted away when she realized her mother had been heartbroken. That she'd been waiting for the man to return to her, and he never did. Was this perhaps the reason that everyday at four o'clock, no matter the weather, her mother had dragged her to the Port of Leith to watch the ships? Was this why her mother searched out the faces of the sailors, especially the ones with hats as extravagant as Santiago's? Because Alesia had thought she was looking for a score, believed the hat meant coin, but it wasn't that at all. Her mother had been searching for the man she loved. The only man she'd allowed to get her with child. Santiago Fernandez.

"Oh, my God." She was going to be sick. Her own name gave a clue as to her parentage... For her middle name was Fern.

"*Sí.* That is she," Santiago said after she revealed her mother's name. "*Bella dama.* What happened to her?"

Alesia could have fainted right then and there. She stumbled backward a step, nearly falling off the rail, save for Thor's arms reaching out to grab her before she tumbled. "But..."

She glanced up at Thor, searching his eyes for something, but not knowing what it was. She couldn't grasp this situation. She swallowed around the lump in her throat. Her vision blurred, throat grew tight. What felt like an attack of panic edged its way along her skin, threatening to take hold. Then Thor touched her face, sliding a gentle finger along her jawline, centering her.

"Dinna fash. I've got ye. 'Tis ye and me against the sea, love."

"Aye." Alesia turned back to Santiago, straightening and summoning the strength in her voice. "My mother died. She died poor, ravaged and bitter. I was a wee lass, helpless in the world, and the only words she had for me on her deathbed were of ye weighing anchor and forgetting about her. But what about me? I had to grow up on my own, fighting for every breath, every moment, every crust of bread." As she railed at the man who'd sired her, the decibels in her voice grew along with the iron in her spine. How long had she waited to shout these words? To let all of this pent-up anger and hurt out? "I fought those who wished to hurt me. Those who wished to use me. Where were ye then? I came here today to tell ye to bugger off. To tell ye that ye're a bastard. A vile devil in human flesh. A curse on ye!" She jabbed her finger at him. "A curse on your whole ship." She whipped a blade from her belt, wrenched it behind her shoulder, and before anyone could stop her, not that they would have, she flung it between the boats.

Time seemed to stand still as everyone watched in sheer disbelief as the knife twisted through the air. As if in slow motion, Santiago tried to duck the coming blow, but he wasn't fast enough, and the blade sank into his arm just above the elbow.

"That's for my mother," Alesia cried. "I dinna care enough about ye to exact my own vengeance. Ye are *nothing* to me."

"You bitch!" Santiago clutched at the dagger in his arm, fury lacing his words and etched in deep grooves on his face.

"Nay, Father," she said evenly, calmly, "*ye're* a bitch, and ye'll die like one, too." At this point, Alesia could no longer stand to look at him. Without a backward glance, she spun on her heel, hopped down from the rail and headed toward the cabin—all the fight gone out of her.

To say Thor was shocked watching Alesia's shoulders sag as she trudged away was an understatement. The lass had been ready for war, covered in weapons. But seeing the man who'd cared so little for her over the past twenty years, who'd abandoned both her and her mother, seemed to have drained the light from her. She was his wee fighter. He couldn't stand to think that the sight of the man before them had drained her of her spark.

Santiago was still sputtering, and Thor wanted to leap from his ship to the Spaniard's deck and pummel him into the planks.

"Could I not just fire one wee cannon, Cap'n?" Edgard said beside him.

Thor grunted a laugh, knowing all of his men felt the same way. The men had come for a fight, and so had he. He'd wanted Santiago and his bastard crew to *feel the wrath of Thor*. But it would seem his specially made cannonballs would not be fired this day. However, they didn't need to fire a cannon to steal the bastard's Spanish gold. The call for the bairn of Santiago had been to bring the child to him, not to hand her over.

"We'll be taking our doubloons," Thor called. "All of it."

Santiago laughed. "You think me such a *idiota*, Captain Thor?"

"I think ye must honor the pirate's code. We did ye a service, and now ye owe us the doubloons as promised."

"*La niña* has aligned with you, Scottish scum. I'll not be honoring anything save seeing the tip of my sword pierce through your *pecho*." He thumped his chest.

"If 'tis a fight ye want, then 'twill be a fight I give ye."

Santiago let out a bellow of agreement, which was all the encouragement Thor needed to launch his attack. With a single word from Thor, Edgard turned to the men and issued orders. Their ship lurched into action. Men climbed the masts and untied the ropes they'd use to swing through the air. The rudder was positioned to the right degree. Rowers pressed their oars into the deep black of the sea, propelling them closer to the Spanish ship and closing the distance of some twenty feet. The wood of their hulls and guns clunked together like lightning and thunder. The Devils of the Deep did not stop as they flew threw the air like crows to land on the deck of *Los Demonios de Mar*.

Shaw, Con and Kelley launched similar attacks on the other two Spanish ships, leaving Santiago to Thor. Likewise, his men ducked from Santiago's sword, swiveled from his bullets, but never struck the man, giving Thor the time he needed to make sure his ship was secure before he, too, joined in the melee.

Gripping a rope with one hand, his claymore in the other, Thor let out his battle cry, one that mirrored that of the warriors from his clan in the Highlands as they went into battle. The haunting sound was enough to give Santiago pause, or maybe to recall where he'd heard a sound like that before.

The man's vacuous eyes met Thor's as he swung through the air and landed with a booming thud on his feet upon the Spanish deck. Swords drawn, the two of them circled each other, determination written on both their faces.

"Come to die, *escoria?*"

Battle waged around them, cannons booming, swords clinking, sparking, fists connecting with flesh. Men grunted with both pain and general excitement. They were a blood-thirsty lot, and this was their game.

Shaw and Kelley had boarded the other two Spanish ships, but Con was swinging toward Santiago's galley, landing with a roll and a swipe at one of the Spanish pirates with a laugh.

"Pardon the interruption," he said with a degree of arrogance as he swatted away one of the Spanish swabs as though the man were no more than a fly. "I but wanted to remind our friend here, dearest Captain Santiago Fernandez, of the mercy I showed his men when I took the *Leucosia*."

"*The Astorga*," Santiago growled.

Con shrugged. "Scum by any other name is still scum."

"English *bastardo*." Santiago spat upon the wood.

"I dinna need Santiago's mercy," Thor interrupted. "I am under no obligation to show him any, and I do not plan to lose."

Con chuckled. "Oh, aye, I know you'd kick his arse into next week. Alas, 'twould be unfair, for Santiago is honor bound to do you no harm given he owes me a favor, after I did not kill his captain. He must give you life in return."

Santiago growled. "*Estoy obligado por honor* not to kill him, however, I can harm him as much as I want."

Con shrugged. "Suit yourself, but I would call a truce if I were you, for Thor does not look as though he will stop at a mere injury."

Thor's chest heaved with indignation and a fiery need to give Santiago a scar to remember him by. Red flashes crossed his eyes when he imagined the pain he'd seen in Alesia's countenance.

"May I make a suggestion?" Alesia's voice cut through the melee, and even the men who'd been fighting on board ceased for a fraction of a second to spot her as she stood upon the rail of the ship's starboard side, still decked out in weapons. When had she gotten there?

Pride pounded in Thor's heart as he beheld her. "By all means, lass."

Santiago looked ready to say something but kept silent.

"A battle with fists. Between the two of ye."

Thor breathed a sigh of relief, half expecting that she would have suggested she fight Santiago herself. While he would have enjoyed seeing her pummel the bastard into the planks, he would have certainly murdered the man if he dared to touch her.

"*Sí,*" Santiago said first. "What are the terms?"

"A fight until one of ye falls and canna get up. But not a fight to the death."

The ship's inhabitants held their breath, waiting for Thor to answer. How the hell could he agree to this? He'd been waiting his entire life for this moment. Had lived and breathed on the image of Santiago's blood. He glanced at Alesia, saw the pleading in her eyes, felt a twinge in his heart. Ballocks, but this was difficult. He was torn between his lust for revenge and the love he felt for her. If he were to disagree, then he'd lose her. But he'd also gain his freedom from bloodlust. Every muscle in him tensed. His enemy so close. What was worse? Betraying his desire for revenge, or betraying his heart and the woman he loved? What would his mother wish for him? An image of her face, of her eyes and smile as she stroked his cheek when he was lad flashed into view. And then he knew. "Agreed."

The men aboard the other ships had also ceased their fighting. A whoosh of exhales mingled with the wind, and one look at Alesia's proud face, and Thor knew he'd made the right choice.

Shaw nodded his approval. Even though Shaw was the

pirate prince of the Devils of the Deep, he had made it known that this was Thor's battle, and he supported Thor's decision.

The ships were called closer, grappling hooks attached to make them practically a single floating city. Men stood on the rails and hung from the ropes as Santiago and Thor both stripped to the waist on the center of the Spanish ship, prepared to fight until one or both of them collapsed. Thor was not going to collapse. Not with Alesia watching. The lass was a fighter, the strongest person, male or female, that he'd ever met. She had determination that rivaled all others. No matter what, he would stand for her, even if he could no longer see, hear or feel, he would remain upright.

Alesia stood between the two of them, a strip of crimson fabric clasped between her fingers as she held it alight. As soon as the fabric left her grip, they would begin.

Thor's heart beat steadily. He was surprisingly calm. For so many years, he'd wanted to rip out Santiago's heart, but now he found himself gaining satisfaction from the notion that he could simply beat the man into a bloody pulp. He'd won the lass. Without Santiago, his heart never would have been as complete as it was now.

With a stomp of her foot and a whistle from her perfect lips, Alesia let the fabric drop and leapt back out of the way to stand beside Edgard.

Santiago wasted no time lunging for Thor. A mistake that would prove his undoing from the beginning. Thor let him. He let the bastard tire himself with every leap forward and every stumble. Thor stepped out of the way, tripped him and kicked him in the arse on his way down. Santiago had sweat dripping from his temples, slicking the skin of his torso, while Thor was barely heated at all.

However, watching the man stumble and fall, as amusing as it was, and as humorous as the brethren found it, was growing tedious. He wanted to be done with it. Upon the man's next growling lunge, Thor punched him square in the jaw, the sound of teeth cracking echoing in his ears.

Santiago stumbled backward, shaking his head, disoriented. But he didn't drop to his knees, though he did wobble.

Thor walked calmly forward, gripped Santiago by the shoulders and put all his force behind head butting the top of his head against Santiago's forehead.

The man fell backward like a sack of grain.

Thor stood over Santiago as he blinked his eyes open, a lump forming in the center of his forehead.

"I wanted to kill ye," Thor said, trying to calm the bloodlust in his veins. "I still want to kill ye. But I willna. Consider this my victory. I want ye to remember upon seeing the bright dawn of every morning, that somewhere on this vast sea is your daughter, and that she is married to me. That your grandchildren will have my blood running through their veins. Let that be cause enough for ye to die a little each day."

Santiago closed his eyes, feigning unconsciousness, but there had been a knowing in his gaze, a hardening. An understanding that showed Thor his words had been heard and comprehended.

A tiny flutter against his hand had Thor looking down. Alesia entwined her fingers with his and raised his arm in the air, letting out a whoop of congratulations.

"Our victor!"

The Pirates of Britannia cheered for Thor, while the *Los Demonios de Mar* grumbled their irritation. A few of them stepped forward, lifted their captain from the planks and carried him out of sight.

"Thank ye," Alesia whispered, leaning up on tiptoe to kiss Thor on the cheek.

"For what?"

177

"For being a man of honor. For being ye. For protecting me."

Thor tugged her into his arms and kissed her properly. And when he pulled back, he said, "Ye bring out the best in me, lass."

"I love ye."

"I love ye with all my heart."

The Devils of the Deep surrounded their captain, still clutching their weapons, muscles tight, and ready to fight any of the Spaniards who might try to retaliate on behalf of their captain, but none stepped forward. In fact, they put their weapons away and held up their hands in surrender.

But surrender was not what Thor wanted. Just the gold. Which he directed Edgard to find and distribute amongst the Scottish and English brethren.

Hand in hand, Thor and Alesia walked to the edge of the ship. Thor lifted her onto the rail and leapt up beside her. He gripped her about the waist with one arm, and held a rope with the other, swinging them back onto the *Leucosia*. The men removed the grappling hooks from the Spanish ships, watching them drift away.

"Are ye ready?" Shaw asked, landing beside them.

"Back to Scarba?"

"Aye," Shaw said with a grin, "but not afore we do one last thing."

"What's that?"

"Make Miss Baird into Mrs. Thor."

Con chuckled as he landed on deck. "Aye, Shaw's got much practice as he married me and Gregg."

Thor looked to Alesia. "What do ye say? Do ye wish to be the mistress of *The Sea Devil*?"

Hope and love and pride shone in her eyes. "Aye, verra much."

He'd thought his chest could not swell with any more happiness, but he found himself surprised.

"I pronounce ye Thor and Alesia, man and wife, Captain and Mistress of *The Sea Devil*," Shaw boomed.

And then Thor kissed her thoroughly.

CHAPTER EIGHTEEN

"Who resides at your castle now?" Alesia languidly ran her fingers in lazy circles over Thor's massive chest.

They'd arrived at the Isle of Scarba, the Devils of the Deep stronghold off the west coast of the Highlands of Scotland. The better part of the last three days had been spent in the cottage house that belonged to Thor on the pirate isle, though they had made an exception to join the brethren in Shaw and Jane's castle for a celebration of their victory and marriage.

Pure joy swelled in Alesia's chest.

"A cousin," Thor said, twirling a tendril of her dark hair around his finger. "Theoretically, I conceded to the next in line, though they all believe I am dead anyhow, so it matters not."

Alesia propped herself up on her elbow and stared at him. "Why do ye not want them to know ye're alive?"

Thor rolled onto his side to face her, his big hand splayed on her hip, tucking her closer. The fire that had been gently crackling let out a little pop that startled her into his arms. Naked breasts crushed to his bare torso. Her husband chuckled, taking the opportunity to scoop her up over his body. Eagerly, she straddled him, liking this position most of all. She enjoyed being in control and watching the way Thor writhed beneath her. Already she could feel him growing hard between her legs, his pulsing flesh pressing against the very heat of her.

"If they knew I was alive, those loyal to my parents would want me to come back and take my place as chief." He shifted slightly beneath her, leaning up to trail his tongue around a turgid pink nipple.

Alesia braced her hands on the muscles of his shoulders, massaging gently as she moved her hips back and forth. She bit her lip, enjoying the friction she created. The pleasure that could be had between the two of them never grew old. If anything, it grew only more intense. Meeting Thor had changed her life in so many ways, but best of all, was that he'd opened her up to hope, happiness and sheer joy.

"And ye dinna want to be chief?" She gasped as his teeth grazed her sensitive flesh.

"Nay, love, I dinna."

"Why?" Alesia gripped the back of his neck, scratching gently in a silent plea for him to quit his teasing and take her nipple into his mouth in earnest.

He gripped her buttocks, the steely bands of his stomach coiling and flexing. Finally, he took a nipple into his mouth. Alesia's head fell back on a moan, fingers tangling with his hair, her question momentarily forgotten.

"I like being a pirate. The brethren are my family. Ye are my family." His breath fanned over her skin as his lips searched out her other nipple, and she arched against him, sighing. "Besides, the sea is my home. Her gentle waves my way of life. I couldna bear it if I were land bound." He shifted beneath her enough that the tip of his arousal pressed to the exact spot she wanted.

Alesia rose a little on her knees, giving him what he desired, and then she sank down, allowing him to fill her. Oh, but it felt so good. Would she ever get over the sensation of being filled? Of the pleasure it brought, the blissful, decadent and wicked sensations it brought over her? *Nay, nay, nay…*

"And ye, love, why do ye ask? Did ye want me to conquer the castle? Capture it just for ye? I would be happy to do it. Ye only need ask."

Rolling her hips back and forth, she looked into his eyes. "The only thing I want ye to conquer is me, in this bed."

Thor chuckled. "But, my *leannan troda*, I like it too much when ye are conquering me."

Alesia wrapped her arms around his neck and quickened her pace. "No matter how we make love," she panted, "never doubt, my love, that it is I who feel conquered."

"Then we conquer each other." He settled his hands back on her hips, gripping firmly as he increased his own pace and held her to match.

Their lips collided, neither one of them able to form words as their bodies took over with determination to reach the final victory—sweet, decadent release.

And when it came, when it shattered them both once more, they collapsed to the mattress together, a mass of tangled, sweat-slickened skin.

"I never would have imagined that happiness, let alone bliss like this, could be mine," Alesia mused, kissing him lightly on the lips.

"Och, *leannan troda*, ye have made me a new man."

"Nay, Thornley MacLeod, ye are still the same man I met some weeks ago. The same one I fell in love with."

He skimmed his hands up her back, leaving gooseflesh in

their wake. "That man would not be lying here now telling ye how much he loves ye."

"Oh, aye, he is." She tickled his ribs. "And I'd not have him lie anywhere else."

"'Tis good ye said it. And that reminds me, Shaw gave me something he found in Edinburgh when he stopped on his way back to Scarba."

"Oh?"

Thor climbed from bed, and she tugged on the sheet to warm herself when the air hit her skin. He walked naked to his desk, giving her a delicious view of his muscled backside. "'Tis quite impressive."

"Aye," she said, smiling at his arse. "'Tis."

Thor turned around and lifted a quizzical brow. "Naughty lass." He pulled a rolled parchment from the desk and brought it over to her. "Read it."

She put her hands on the parchment, and bit her lip. "I canna read well, Thor. I…know how to read a few things, enough to keep me alive, but not well enough to read this letter."

"'Tis not a letter, love. And I'll help ye read anything ye dinna know the meaning of. In fact, I'll teach ye how to read everything if ye wish." He settled down beside her.

"Thank ye." She nodded, blushing, never having considered that her lack of literacy would be something she should be embarrassed about. But he wasn't judging her. There was no censure, only love.

Alesia took her time unrolling the parchment and it revealed a word she knew well—*WANTED*.

Below the word was a drawing that was quite a good match to her own face.

"'Tis me."

"Aye, love."

"Wanted… Och, no! They meant to hang me when I boarded your ship. They will be looking for me."

Thor laughed. "Trust me, my *leannan troda*, they shall never have ye." He tapped some words below her portrait. "Can ye read that?"

She squinted her eyes, making out the letters and moving her tongue around her mouth, but she was unable to form the sounds that they might mean. "Tell me, please."

"They call ye the Wharf Wench."

Alesia giggled, not in the least put out. "That is a grand improvement from wharf rat."

"Aye, but I was thinking I might need to send them a correction." Thor moved to all fours, crawling toward her, over her, pinning her to the bed.

"Oh?" The parchment fell away, for whenever he was this close to her, or far away, she longed to touch him, to feel his heated skin beneath her fingertips.

"Aye, for ye're no wench, ye're a pirate now."

"And proud of it." She flicked the parchment to the floor, determined to set it on fire later when she finally climbed out of bed. "Perhaps I ought to introduce them to my new identity."

Thor nuzzled her neck, nipped at her earlobe. "How do ye propose doing that?"

"Well"—she slid a foot up and down his calf—"I happen to know for a fact that there is a shipment of whisky that comes straight down the channel from the Highlands to be unloaded at Leith every Thursday morn."

"And ye propose we steal it." His mouth traveled the length of her neck, and then back up to her ear.

"At sea, of course, but we can give them a message to relay to the guards at the dock." She tugged his beard until he pressed his lips to hers.

"Ah, a most excellent plan," he murmured against her mouth.

"And the whisky"—she bit his lower lip gently—"we can distribute to the brethren."

"Ye're so verra generous. But what of the clans in the north providing the whisky who have done us no harm?" Thor's big hand braced on the side of her thigh, sliding beneath her knee and lifting to settle himself firmly between her hips, where already she felt him ready to take her once more.

"I didna think about that." She slid her arms around his middle and lifted her hips. "Perhaps we can send them enough of Santiago's gold to cover the cost."

"Your gold." He plunged into her, and for a moment, both of them were caught up in the sheer pleasure of being one.

"Aye. The gold," she moaned. "There's plenty of it, and I rather like the idea of paying the innocent and playing tricks on the blackguards who mistreated me my whole life."

Thor wrapped her up in his arms, and pressed his forehead to hers. "I am going to love having a lifetime of adventures with ye."

"Och, but, ye sea devil, we've already started."

And then they left their plans for another time, for there was only one adventure they wanted to embark on at the moment—each other.

If you enjoyed THE SEA DEVIL, please spread the word by leaving a review on the site where you purchased your copy, or a reader site such as Goodreads or Shelfari! I love to hear from readers too, so drop me a line at authorelizaknight@gmail.com *OR visit me on Facebook:* https://www.facebook.com/elizaknightauthor*. I'm also on Twitter: @ElizaKnight. If you'd like to receive my*

occasional newsletter, please sign up at <u>www.</u>
<u>elizaknight.com.</u> *Many thanks!*

HAVE YOU READ SAVAGE OF THE SEA, THE FIRST BOOK IN THE
Devils of the Deep, Pirates of Britannia series? Check out this
excerpt!

Edinburgh Castle, Scotland
November 1440

Shaw MacDougall stood in the great hall of Edinburgh
Castle with dread in the pit of his stomach. He was amongst
dozens of other armored knights—though he was no knight.
Nay, he was a blackmailed pirate under the guise of a merce-
nary for the day. And though he'd not known the job he was
hired to do until he arrived at the castle, and still didn't
really. He'd been told to wait until given an order, and ever
since, the leather-studded armor weighed heavily on him,
and sweat dripped in a steady line down his spine.

The wee King of Scotland, just ten summers, sat at the
dais entertaining his guests, who were but children themselves. William Douglas, Earl of Douglas, was only sixteen,
and his brother was only a year or two older than the king
himself. Beside the lads was a beautiful young lass, with long
golden locks that caught the light of the torches. The lass
was perhaps no more than sixteen herself, though she
already had a woman's body—a body he should most
certainly *not* be looking at. And though he was only a
handful of years over twenty, and might be convinced she
was of age, he was positive she was far too young for him.
Wide blue eyes flashed from her face and held the gaze of
everyone in the room just long enough that they were left

squirming. And her mouth… God, she had a mouth made to—

Ballocks! It was wrong to look at her in any way that might be construed as…desire.

There was an air of innocence about her that clashed with the cynical look she sometimes cast the earl, whom Shaw had guessed might be her husband. It wasn't hard to spot a woman unhappily married. Hell, it was a skill he'd honed while in port, as he loved to dally with disenchanted wives and leave them quite satisfied.

Unfortunately for him, he was not interested in wee virginal lasses. And so, would not be leaving *that* lass satisfied. Decidedly, he kept his gaze averted from her and eyed the men about the room.

Torches on the perimeter walls lit the great hall, but only dimly. None of the candelabras were burning, leaving many parts of the room cast in shadow—the corners in particular. And for Shaw, this was quite disturbing.

He was no stranger to battle—and not just any type of battle—he was intimately acquainted with guerilla warfare, the *pirate* way. But why the hell would he, the prince of pirates, be hired by a noble lord intimately acquainted with the king?

Shaw glanced sideways at the man who'd hired him. Sir Andrew Livingstone. Shaw's payment wasn't in coin, nay, he'd taken this mission in exchange for several members of his crew being released from the dungeons without a trial. Had he not, they'd likely have hung. Shaw had been more than happy to strike a bargain with Livingstone in exchange for his men's lives.

Now, he dreaded the thought of what that job might be.

This would be the last time he let his men convince him mooring in Blackness Bay for a night of debauchery was a good idea. It was there that two of his crew had decided to act like drunken fools, and it was also there, that half a dozen other pirates jumped in to save them. They'd all been arrested and brought before Livingstone, who'd tossed them in a cell.

And now, here he was, feeling out of place in the presence of the king and the two men, Livingstone and the Lord Chancellor, who had arranged for this oddly dark feast. They kept giving each other strange looks, as though speaking through gestures. Shaw shifted, cracking his neck, and glanced back at the dais table lined with youthful nobles.

Seated beside the young earl, the lass glanced furtively around the room, her eyes jumpy as a rabbit as though she sensed something. She sipped her cup daintily and picked at the food on her plate, peeking nervously about the room. Every once in a while, she'd give her head a little shake as if trying to convince herself that whatever it was she sensed was all in her head.

The air in the room shifted, growing tenser. There was a subtle nod from the Lord Chancellor to a man near the back of the room, who then disappeared. At the same time, a knight approached the lass with a message. She wrinkled her nose, glancing back toward the young lad to her left and shaking her head, dismissing the knight. But a second later, she was escorted, rather unwillingly, from the room.

Shaw tensed at the way the knight gripped her arm and that her idiotic boy husband didn't seem to care at all. What was the meaning of all this?

Perhaps the reason presented itself a moment later. A man dressed in black from head to toe, including a hood covering his face, entered from the rear of the great hall carrying a blackened boar's head on a platter. He walked slowly, and as those sitting at the table turned their gaze toward him, their eyes widened. In what though? Shock? Curiosity? Or was it fear?

Did Livingstone plan to kill the king?

If so, why did none of the guards pull out their swords to stop this messenger of death?

Shaw was finding it difficult to stand by and let this happen.

But the man in black did not stop in front of the king. Instead, he stopped in front of the young earl and his wee brother, placing the boar's head between them. Shaw knew what it meant before either of the victims it was served to did.

"Nay," he growled under his breath.

The two lads looked at the blackened head with disgust, and then the earl seemed to recognize the menacing gesture. Glowering at the servant, he said, "Get that bloody thing out of my sight."

Shaw was taken aback that the young man spoke with such authority, though he supposed at sixteen, he himself had already captained one of MacAlpin's ships and posed that same authority.

At this, Livingstone and Crichton stood and took their places before the earl and his brother.

"William Douglas, sixth Earl of Douglas, and Sir David Douglas, ye're hereby charged with treason against His Majesty King James II."

The young king worked hard to hide his surprise, sitting up a little taller. "What? Nay!"

The earl glanced at the king with a sneer one gives a child they think deserves punishment. "What charges could ye have against us?" Douglas shouted. "We've done nothing wrong. We are loyal to our king."

"Ye stand before your accusers and deny the charges?" Livingstone said, eyebrow arched, his tone brooking no argument.

"*What* charges?" Douglas's face had turned red with rage, and he stood, hands fisted at his sides.

Livingstone slammed his hands down on the table in front of Douglas. "Guilty. Ye're guilty."

William Douglas jerked to a stand, shoving his brother behind him, and pulled his sword from its scabbard. "Lies!" He lunged forward and would have been able to do damage to his accusers if not for the seasoned warriors who overpowered him from behind.

"Stop," King James shouted, his small voice drowned out by the screams of the Douglas lads and the shouts of the warriors.

Quickly overpowered, the noble lads were dragged kicking and screaming from the great hall, all while King James shouted for the spectacle to cease.

Shaw was about to follow the crowd outside when Livingstone gripped his arm.

"Take care of Lady Douglas."

Lady Douglas. The sixteen-year-old countess.

"Take care?" Shaw needed to hear it explicitly.

"Aye. Execute her. I dinna care how. Just see it done." The man shrugged. "We were going to let her live, but I've changed my mind. Might as well get her out of the way, too."

Livingstone wanted Shaw to kill her? As though it was acceptable for a lord to execute lads on trumped up charges of treason, but the murder of a lass, that was a pirate's duty.

Shaw ground his teeth and nodded. Killing innocent lassies wasn't part of his code. He'd never done so before and didn't want to start now. Blast it all! Six pirates for one wee lass. One beautiful, enchanting lass who'd never done him harm. Hell, he didn't even know her. Slipping unnoticed past the bloodthirsty crowd wasn't hard given they were too intent on the insanity unfolding around them. He made his way toward the arch where he'd seen the lass dragged too not a quarter hour before.

The arch led to a dimly lit rounded staircase and the only way to go was up. Pulling his *sgian-dubh* from his boot, Shaw hurried up the stairs, his soft boots barely a whisper on every stone step. At the first round, he encountered a closed door. An ear pressed against the wood proved no one inside. He went up three more stairs to another quiet room. He continued to climb, listening at every door until he reached the very top. The door was closed, and it was quiet, but the air was charged making the hair on the back of his neck prickle.

Taking no more time, Shaw shouldered the door open to find the knight who'd escorted the lass from the great hall lying on top of her on the floor. They struggled. Her legs were parted, skirts up around her hips, tears of rage on her reddened face. The bastard had a hand over her mouth and sneered up at Shaw upon his entry.

Fury boiled inside him. Shaw slammed the door shut so hard it rattled the rafters.

"Get up," Shaw demanded, rage pummeling through him at having caught the man as he tried to rape the lass.

Tears streamed from her eyes, which blazed blue as she stared at him. Her face was pale, and her limbs were trembling. Still, there was defiance in the set of her jaw. Something inside his chest clenched. He wanted to rip the whoreson limb from limb. And he knew for a fact he wasn't going to kill Lady Douglas.

"I said get up." Shaw advanced a step or two, averting his eyes for a moment as the knight removed himself from her person, letting her adjust her skirts down her legs.

Shaw waved his hand at her, indicating she should run from the room, but rather than escape, she went to the corner of the chamber and cowered.

Saints, but his heart went out to her.

Shaw was a pirate, had witnessed a number of savage acts, and the one thing he could never abide by was the rape of a woman.

The knight didn't speak, instead he charged toward Shaw with murder in his eyes.

But that didn't matter. Shaw had dealt with a number of men like him who were used to preying on women. He would be easy, and he would bear the entire brutal brunt of Shaw's ire.

Shaw didn't move, simply waiting the breath it took for the knight to be on him. He leapt to the left, out of the path of the knight's blade, and sank his own blade in quick succession into the man's gut, then heart, then neck. Three rapid jabs.

The knight fell to the ground, blood pouring from his wounds, his eyes and mouth wide in surprise. Too easy.

"Please," the lass whimpered from the corner. The defiance that had shown on her face before disappeared, and now she only looked frightened. "Please, dinna hurt me."

"I would never. Ye have my word." Shaw tried to make his words soothing, but they came out so gruff, he was certain they were exactly the opposite.

He wiped the blood from his blade onto the knight's hose and then stuck the *sgian-dubh* back into his boot. He approached the lass, hands outstretched, as he might a wild filly. "We must go, lass."

"Please, go." She wiped at the blood on her lips. "Leave me here."

"Lady Jane, is that right?" he asked, ignoring her plea for him to leave her.

She nodded.

"I need to get ye out of here. I was..." Should he tell her?

"I was sent by Livingstone to…take your life. But I willna. I swear it. Come now, we must escape."

"What?" Her tears ceased in her surprise.

"Ye canna be seen. The lads, your husband…" Shaw ran a hand through his hair. "Livingstone willna let them leave alive. He doesna want *ye* to leave alive."

That defiance returned to her striking blue eyes as she stared him down. "I dinna believe ye."

"Trust me."

She shook her head and slid slowly up the wall to stand, her hands braced on the stone behind her. "Where is my husband?"

Shaw grimaced. "He's gone, lass. Come now, or ye'll be gone soon, too." He'd not been hired for this task, to take a shaking lass out of castle and hide her away. But the alternative was much worse. And he'd not be committing the murder of an innocent today.

Indeed, he risked his entire reputation by being here and doing anything at all, but he was pretty certain the two lads she'd arrived with were dead already, and along with them the rest of their party. Livingstone and Crichton weren't about to let the lass live to tell the tale or rally the rest of the Douglas clan to come after them. That line was healthy, long and powerful.

"I dinna understand," she mumbled. "Who are ye?"

"I am Shaw MacDougall."

She searched his eyes, seeking understanding and not finding it. "I dinna know ye."

"All ye need to know is I am here to get ye to safety. Come now. They'll be looking for ye soon." And him. This was a direct breach of their contract, and Livingstone would not stop until he had Shaw's head on a spike.

But Shaw didn't care. He hated the bastard and had been looking for retribution. Let that be a lesson to Livingstone for attempting to blackmail a pirate. His men would be proud to know he'd not succumbed to the blackguard's demands. As he stood there, they were already being broken out of the jail at Blackness Bay.

Stopping a few feet in front of the lass, he held out his hand and gestured for her to take it. She shook her head.

"Lady Jane, I canna begin to understand what ye're feeling right now, but I also canna stress enough the urgency of the situation. I've a horse, and my ship is not far from here. Come now, else surrender your fate to that of your husband."

"William."

"He is dead, lass. Or soon to be."

"Nay…" Her chin wobbled, and she looked ready to collapse.

"Aye. There is no time to argue. Come. I will carry ye if ye need me to."

Perhaps it would be better if he simply lifted her up and tossed her over his shoulder. Shaw made a move to reach for her when she shook her head and straightened her shoulders.

"Will ye take me to Iona, Sir MacDougall?"

"Aye. Will Livingstone know to look for ye there?"

She shook her head. "My aunt is a nun there. Livingstone may put it together at some point, but I will be safe there for now."

"Aye."

"Oh…" She started to tremble uncontrollably. "Oh my… I… I'm going to…" And then she fell into his arms, unconscious.

Shaw let out a sigh and tossed her over his shoulder as he'd thought to do just a few moments before. Hopefully, she'd not wake until they were on his ship and had already set sail. He sneaked back down the stairs, and rather than go out the front where he could hear screams of pain and shouts filled with the thirst for blood, he snuck her out the postern gate at the back of the castle. He half ran, half slid down the steep slope, thanking the heavens every second when the lass did not waken.

Though he'd arrived at the castle on a horse, he'd had one of his men ride with another and instructed him to wait at the bottom of the castle hill in case he needed to make an escape. Some might say he had a sixth sense about such things, but he preferred to say that he simply had a pirate's sense of preservation.

Livingstone was a blackguard who'd made a deal with a pirate to commit murder. A powerful lord only made dealings with a pirate when he needed muscle at his back. And when he chose to keep his own hands clean. But that didn't mean Livingstone wouldn't hesitate killing Shaw.

Well, Livingstone was a fool. And Shaw was not. There was his horse waiting for him at the bottom of the hill just as he'd asked.

"Just as ye said, Cap'n," Jack, his quartermaster—called so for being a Jack-of-all-trades—said with a wide, toothy grin. "What's that?"

Shaw raised a brow, glancing at the rounded feminine arse beside his face. "A lass. Let's go."

"Oh, taken to kidnapping now, aye?"

"Not exactly." Shaw tossed the lass up onto the horse and climbed up behind her. "Come on, Jack. Back to the ship."

They took off at a canter, loping through the dirt-packed roads of Edinburgh toward the Water of Leith that led out to the Firth of Forth and the sea beyond. But then on second thought, he veered his horse to the right. When they rowed their skiff up the Leith to get to the castle, they'd had more time. Now, time was of the essence, and riding their horses straight to the docks at the Forth where his ship awaited would be quicker. No doubt, as soon as Livingstone noticed

Shaw was gone—as well as the girl—he'd send a horde of men after him. Shaw could probably convince a few of them to join his crew, but he didn't have time for that.

A quarter of an hour later, their horses covered in a sheen of sweat, Shaw shouted for his men to lower the gangplank, and he rode the horse right up onto the main deck of the *Savage of the Sea*, his pride and joy, the ship he'd captained since he was not much older than the lass he carried.

"Avast ye, maties! All hands hoy! Weigh anchor and hoist the mizzen. Ignore the wench and get us the hell out of here. To Iona we sail!" With his instructions given, Shaw carried the still unconscious young woman up the few stairs to his own quarters, pushing open the door and slamming it shut behind him.

There, he paused. If he set her on the bed, what would she think when she woke? What would he think if he saw her there? She was much too young for him, aye. But whenever he brought a wench to his quarters and laid her on the bed, it was not for any bit of *saving*, unless it was release from the tension pleasure built.

And yet, the floor did not seem like a good spot, either.

He settled for the long wooden bench at the base of his bed.

As soon as he laid her there, her eyes popped open, and she leapt to her feet. "What are ye doing? Where have ye taken me?" She looked about her wildly, reaching for nothing and everything at once. Blond locks flying wildly.

"Calm yourself, lass." Shaw raised a sardonic brow. "We sail for Iona as ye requested. And from there, we shall part ways."

She eyed him suspiciously. "And nothing more?"

He crossed his arms over his chest and studied her. As the seconds ticked past, her shoulders seemed to sag a little more, and that crazed look evaporated from her eyes.

"Nothing save the satisfaction that I have taken ye from a man who would have done ye harm."

"Livingstone?"

"Aye."

Her lower lip trembled. "Aye. He will want to kill all who bear the Douglas name."

Shaw's eyes lowered to her flat belly. "Might there be another?" he asked.

She shook her head violently. "Ye saved me just before that awful man could…"

"Ye misunderstand me, my lady. I meant your husband's…" Ballocks, why did he find it hard to say the word *seed* to the lass? He was a bloody pirate and far more vulgar words, to any number of wenches, had come from his mouth.

She lifted her chin, jutting it forward obstinately. "There is nothing."

Shaw chose to take her word for it rather than discuss the intimate relationship she might have had with her boy husband and when the last time her courses had come. "Then ye need only worry about your own neck, and no one else's."

He expected her to fall into a puddle of tears, but she didn't.

The lass simply nodded and then said, "I owe ye a debt, Sir MacDougall."

"Call me Savage, lass. And rest assured, I will collect."

Read more of *Savage of the Sea*!

Don't miss out on Eliza Knight's new and exciting series — Prince Charlie's Angels, starting with Book One: *The Rebel Wears Plaid*!

. . .

THESE HEROINES RISK THEIR LIVES TO PROTECT JACOBITE **soldiers. Hiding them, healing their wounds, and aiding in their escape from enemy forces, puts these fiery ladies in harm's way, but their loyalty wins out over fear every time.**

TORAN FRASER IS HELL-BENT ON TAKING DOWN THE Jacobites. On a late-night mission, he's intercepted by a woman known only as "Mistress J" who's determined to put Prince Charlie back on the throne of Scotland. Toran can't resist her appeal—especially with her pistol pointed at his heart—and suddenly finds himself joining the rebellion...

BY DAY, HIGHBORN JENNY MACKINTOSH RUNS HER ESTATE IN the Highlands. By night, she raises coin, delivers weapons, and recruits soldiers for the Jacobite rebellion. When she encounters a handsome Highlander who is clearly on the run, she is more than a little intrigued. She isn't expecting to become the target of his sworn enemy...

"THE REBEL WEARS PLAID IS FABULOUS—BOLD, adventurous, and brimming with intrigue and memorable characters."--Cathy Maxwell, New York Times bestselling author

"AN ADMIRABLY COURAGEOUS HEROINE, A WONDERFULLY HOT hero, impeccable history, well-crafted characters, and edge-of-your-seat adventure makes this Highland romance irresistible. An excellent beginning to an engrossing series. I can't wait for the next one!" --*New York Times* bestselling author Jennifer Ashley

"OUTLANDER FANS WILL BE THRILLED BY ELIZA KNIGHT'S perfect mix of history and romance."—Jennifer McQuiston, *New York Times* bestselling author

"THE INTRIGUE AND HISTORICAL DETAILS ARE CAPTIVATING, BUT readers should be prepared for an excruciatingly slow burn in the love story, which remains relatively understated for a large chunk of the novel. Fans of strong female protagonists and subtle passion will be pleased." --*Publisher's Weekly*

ABOUT THE AUTHOR

Eliza Knight is an award-winning and *USA Today* bestselling indie author of over fifty sizzling historical romance and erotic romance. Under the name E. Knight, she pens rip-your-heart-out historical fiction. While not reading, writing or researching for her latest book, she chases after her three children. In her spare time (if there is such a thing…) she likes daydreaming, wine-tasting, traveling, hiking, staring at the stars, watching movies, shopping and visiting with family and friends. She lives atop a small mountain with her own knight in shining armor, three princesses and two very naughty puppies. Visit Eliza at http://www.elizaknight.comor her historical blog History Undressed: www.historyundressed.com. Sign up for her newsletter to get news about books, events, contests and sneak peaks! http://eepurl.com/CSFFD

facebook.com/elizaknightfiction

twitter.com/elizaknight

instagram.com/elizaknightfiction

bookbub.com/authors/eliza-knight

goodreads.com/elizaknight

pinterest.com/authoreknight

EXCERPT FROM THE HIGHLANDER'S GIFT

CHAPTER ONE

Dupplin Castle
Scottish Highlands
Winter, 1318

Sir Niall Oliphant had lost something.

Not a trinket, or a boot. Not a pair of hose, or even his favorite mug. Nothing as trivial as that. In fact, he wished it *was* so minuscule that he could simply replace it. What'd he'd lost was devastating, and yet it felt entirely selfish given some of those closest to him had lost their lives.

He was still here, living and breathing. He was still walking around on his own two feet. Still handsome in the face. Still able to speak coherently, even if he didn't want to.

But he couldn't replace what he'd lost.

What he'd lost would irrevocably change his life, his entire future. It made him want to back into the darkest corner and let his life slip away, to forget about even having a future at all. To give everything he owned to his brother and say goodbye. He was useless now. Unworthy.

Niall cleared the cobwebs that had settled in his throat by slinging back another dram of whisky. The shutters in his darkened bedchamber were closed tight, the fire long ago grown cold. He didn't allow candles in the room, nor visitors. So when a knock sounded at his door, he ignored it, preferring to chug his spirits from the bottle rather than pouring it into a cup.

The knocking grew louder, more insistent.

"Go away," he bellowed, slamming the whisky down on the side table beside where he sat, and hearing the clay jug shatter. A shard slid into his finger, stinging as the liquor splashed over it. But he didn't care.

This pain, pain in his only index finger, he wanted to have. Wanted a reminder there was still some part of him left. Part of him that could still feel and bleed. He tried to ignore that part of him that wanted to be alive, however small it was.

The handle on the door rattled, but Niall had barred it the day before. Refusing anything but whisky. Maybe he could drink himself into an oblivion he'd never wake from. Then all of his worries would be gone forever.

"Niall, open the bloody door."

The sound of his brother's voice through the cracks had Niall's gaze widening slightly. Walter was a year younger than he was. And still whole. Walter had tried to understand Niall's struggle, but what man could who'd not been through it himself?

"I said go away, ye bloody whoreson." His words slurred, and he went to tipple more of the liquor only to recall he'd just shattered it everywhere.

Hell and damnation. The only way to get another bottle would be to open the door.

"I'll pretend I didna hear ye just call our dear mother a whore. Open the damned door, or I'll take an axe to it."

Like hell he would. Walter was the least aggressive one in their family. Sweet as a lad, he'd grown into a strong warrior, but he was also known as the heart of the Oliphant clan. The idea of him chopping down a door was actually funny. Outside, the corridor grew silent, and Niall leaned his head back against the chair, wondering how long he had until his brother returned, and if it was enough time to sneak down to the cellar and get another jug of whisky.

Needless to say, when a steady thwacking sounded at the door—reminding Niall quite a bit like the heavy side of an axe—he sat up straighter and watched in drunken fascination as the door started to splinter. Shards of wood came flying through the air as the hole grew larger and the sound of the axe beating against the surface intensified.

Walter had grown some bloody ballocks.

Incredible.

Didn't matter. What would Walter accomplish by breaking down the door? What could he hope would happen?

Niall wasn't going to leave the room or accept food.

Niall wasn't going to move on with his life.

So he sat back and waited, curious more than anything as to what Walter's plan would be once he'd gained entry.

Just as tall and broad of shoulder as Niall, Walter kicked through the remainder of the door and ducked through the ragged hole.

"That's enough." Walter looked down at Niall, his face fierce, reminding him very much of their father when they were lads.

"That's enough?" Niall asked, trying to keep his eyes wide but having a hard time. The light from the corridor gave his brother a darkened, shadowy look.

"Ye've sat in this bloody hell hole for the past three days." Walter gestured around the room. "Ye stink of shite. Like a bloody pig has laid waste to your chamber."

"Are ye calling me a shite pig?" Niall thought about standing up, calling his brother out, but that seemed like too much effort.

"Mayhap I am. Will it make ye stand up any faster?"

Niall pursed his lips, giving the impression of actually considering it. "Nay."

"That's what I thought. But I dinna care. Get up."

Niall shook his head slowly. "I'd rather not."

"I'm not asking."

My, my. Walter's ballocks were easily ten times than Niall had expected. The man was bloody testing him to be sure.

"Last time I checked, I was the eldest," Niall said.

"Ye might have been born first, but ye lost your mind some time ago, which makes me the better fit for making decisions."

Niall hiccupped. "And what decisions would ye be making, wee brother?"

"Getting your arse up. Getting ye cleaned up. Airing out the gongheap."

"Doesna smell so bad in here." Niall gave an exaggerated sniff, refusing to admit that Walter was indeed correct. It smelled horrendous.

"I'm gagging, brother. I might die if I have to stay much longer."

"Then by all means, pull up a chair."

"Ye're an arse."

"No more so than ye."

"Not true."

Niall sighed heavily. "What do ye want? Why would ye make me leave? I've nothing to live for anymore."

"Ye've eight-thousand reasons to live, ye blind goat."

"Eight thousand?"

"A random number." Walter waved his hand and kicked at something on the floor. "Ye've the people of your clan, the warriors ye lead, your family. The woman ye're betrothed to marry. Everyone is counting on ye, and ye must come out of here and attend to your duties. Ye've mourned long enough."

"How can ye presume to tell me that I've mourned long enough? Ye know nothing." A slow boiling rage started in Niall's chest. All these men telling him how to feel. All these men thinking they knew better. A bunch of bloody ballocks!

"Aye, I've not lost what ye have, brother. Ye're right. I dinna know what 'tis like to be ye, either. But I know what 'tis like to be the one down in the hall waiting for ye to come and take care of your business. I know what 'tis like to look upon the faces of the clan as they worry about whether they'll be raided or ravaged while their leader sulks in a vat of whisky and does nothing to care for them."

Niall gritted his teeth. No one understood. And he didn't need the reminder of his constant failings.

"Then take care of it," Niall growled, jerking forward fast enough that his vision doubled. "Ye've always wanted to be first. Ye've always wanted what was mine. Go and have it. Have it all."

Walter took a step back as though Niall had hit him. "How can ye say that?" Even in the dim light, Niall could see the pain etched on his brother's features. Aye, what he'd said was a lie, but it had made him feel better all the same.

"Ye heard me. Get the fuck out." Niall moved to push himself from the chair, remembered too late how difficult that would be, and fell back into it. Instead, he let out a string of curses that had Walter shaking his head.

"Ye need to get yourself together, decide whether or not ye are going to turn your back on this clan. Do it for yourself. Dinna go down like this. Ye are still Sir Niall fucking

Oliphant. Warrior. Heir to the chiefdom of Oliphant. Hero. Leader. Brother. Soon to be husband and father."

Walter held his gaze unwaveringly. A torrent of emotion jabbed from that dark look into Niall's chest, crushing his heart.

"Get out," he said again through gritted teeth, feeling the pain of rejecting his brother acutely.

They'd always been so close. And even though he was pushing him away, he also desperately wanted to pull him closer.

He wanted to hug him tightly, to tell him not to worry, that soon enough he'd come out of the dark and be the man Walter once knew. But those were all lies, for he would never be the same again, and he couldn't see how he would ever be able to exit this room and attempt a normal life.

"Ye're not the only one who's lost a part of himself," Walter muttered as he ducked beneath the door. "I want my brother back."

"Your brother is dead."

At that, Walter paused. He turned back around, a snarl poised on his lips, and Niall waited longingly for whatever insult would come out. Any chance to engage in a fight, but then Walter's face softened. "Maybe he is."

With those soft words uttered, he disappeared, leaving behind the gaping hole and the shattered wood on the floor, a haunting mirror image to the wide-open wound Niall felt in his soul.

Niall glanced down to his left, at the sleeve that hung empty at his side, a taunting reminder of his failure in battle. Warrior. Ballocks! Not even close.

When he considered lying down on the ground and licking the whisky from the floor, he knew it was probably time to leave his chamber. But he was no good to anyone outside of his room. Perhaps he could prove that fact once and for all, then Walter would leave him be. And he knew his brother spoke the truth about smelling like a pig. He'd not bathed in days. If he was going to prove he was worthless as a leader now, he would do so smelling decent, so people took him seriously rather than believing him to be mad.

Slipping through the hole in the door, he walked noiselessly down the corridor to the stairs at the rear used by the servants, tripping only once along the way. He attempted to steal down the winding steps, a feat that nearly had him breaking his neck. In fact, he took the last dozen steps on his arse. Once he reached the entrance to the side of the bailey, he lifted the bar and shoved the door open, the cool wind a welcome blast against his heated skin. With the sun set, no one saw him creep outside and slink along the stone as he made his way to the stables and the massive water trough kept for the horses. He might as well bathe there, like the animal he was.

Trough in sight, he staggered forward and tumbled head-first into the icy water.

Niall woke sometime later, still in the water, but turned over at least. He didn't know whether to be grateful he'd not drowned. His clothes were soaked, and his legs hung out on either side of the wooden trough. It was still dark, so at least he'd not slept through the night in the chilled water.

He leaned his head back, body covered in wrinkled gooseflesh and teeth chattering, and stared up at the sky. Stars dotted the inky-black landscape and swaths of clouds streaked across the moon, as if one of the gods had swiped his hand through it, trying to wipe it away. But the moon was steadfast. Silver and bright and ever present. Returning as it should each night, though hiding its beauty day after day until it was just a sliver that made one wonder if it would return.

What was he doing out here? Not just in the tub freezing

his idiot arse off, but here in this world? Why hadn't he been taken? Why had only part of him been stolen? Cut away…

Niall shuddered, more from the memory of that moment when his enemy's sword had cut through his armor, skin, muscle and bone. The crunching sound. The incredible pain.

He squeezed his eyes shut, forcing the memories away.

This is how he'd been for the better part of four months. Stumbling drunk and angry about the castle when he wasn't holed up in his chamber. Yelling at his brother, glowering at his father and mother, snapping at anyone who happened to cross his path. He'd become everything he hated.

There had been times he'd thought about ending it all. He always came back to the simple question that was with him now as he stared up at the large face of the moon.

"Why am I still here?" he murmured.

"Likely because ye havena pulled your arse out of the bloody trough."

Walter.

Niall's gaze slid to the side to see his brother standing there, arms crossed over his chest. "Are ye my bloody shadow? Come to tell me all my sins?"

"When will ye see I'm not the enemy? I want to help."

Niall stared back up at the moon, silently asking what he should do, begging for a sign.

Walter tugged at his arm. "Come on. Get out of the trough. Ye're not a pig as much as ye've been acting the part. Let us get ye some food."

Niall looked over at his little brother, perhaps seeing him for the first time. His throat felt tight, closing in on itself as a well of emotion overflowed from somewhere deep in his gut.

"Why do ye keep trying to help me? All I've done is berate ye for it."

"Aye. That's true, but I know ye speak from pain. Not from your heart."

"I dinna think I have a heart left."

Walter rolled his eyes and gave a swift tug, pulling him halfway from the trough. Though Niall was weak from lack of food and too much whisky, he managed to get himself the rest of the way out. He stood in the moonlight, dripping water around the near frozen ground.

"Ye have a heart. Ye have a soul. One arm. That is all ye've lost. Ye still have your manhood, aye?"

Niall shrugged. Aye, he still had his bloody cock, but what woman wanted a decrepit man heaving overtop of her with his mangled body in full view.

"I know what ye're thinking," Walter said. "And the answer is, every eligible maiden and all her friends. Not to mention the kitchen wenches, the widows in the glen, and their sisters."

"Ballocks," Niall muttered.

"Ye're still handsome. Ye're still heir to a powerful clan. Wake up, man. This is not ye. Ye canna let the loss of your arm be the destruction of your whole life. Ye're not the first man to ever be maimed in battle. Dinna be a martyr."

"Says the man with two arms."

"Ye want me to cut it off? I'll bloody do it." Walter turned in a frantic circle as if looking for the closest thing with a sharp edge.

Niall narrowed his eyes, silent, watching, waiting. When had his wee brother become such an intense force? Walter marched toward the barn, hand on the door, yanked it wide as if to continue the blockhead search. Niall couldn't help following after his brother who marched forward with purpose, disappearing inside the barn.

A flutter of worry dinged in Niall's stomach. Walter wouldn't truly go through with something so stupid, would he?

When he didn't immediately reappear, Niall's pang of

worry heightened into dread. Dammit, he just might. With all the changes Walter had made recently, there was every possibility that he'd gone mad. Well, Niall might wish to disappear, but not before he made certain his brother was all right.

With a groan, Niall lurched forward, grabbed the door and yanked it open. The stables were dark and smelled of horses, leather and hay. He could hear a few horses nickering, and the soft snores of the stable hands up on the loft fast asleep.

"Walter," he hissed. "Enough. No more games."

Still, there was silence.

He stepped farther into the barn, and the door closed behind him, blocking out all the light save for a few strips that sank between cracks in the roof.

His feet shuffled silently on the dirt floor. Where the bloody hell had his brother gone?

And why was his heart pounding so fiercely? He trudged toward the first set of stables, touching the wood of the gates. A horse nudged his hand with its soft muzzle, blowing out a soft breath that tickled his palm, and Niall's heart squeezed.

"Prince," he whispered, leaning his forehead down until he felt it connect with the warm, solidness of his warhorse. Prince nickered and blew out another breath.

Niall had not ridden in months. If not for his horse, he might be dead. But rather than be irritated Prince had done his job, he felt nothing but pride that the horse he'd trained from a colt into a mammoth had done his duty.

After Niall's arm had been severed and he was left for dead, Prince had nudged him awake, bent low and nipped at Niall's legs until he'd managed to crawl and heave himself belly first over the saddle. Prince had taken him home like that, a bleeding sack of grain.

Having thought him dead, the clan had been shocked and

surprised to see him return, and that's when the true battle for his life had begun. He'd lost so much blood, succumbed to fever, and stopped breathing more than once. Hell, it was a miracle he was still alive.

Which begged the question—*why, why, why…*

"He's missed ye." Walter was beside him, and Niall jerked toward his brother, seeing his outline in the dark.

"Is that why ye brought me in here?"

"Did ye really think I'd cut off my arm?" Walter chuckled. "Ye know I like to fondle a wench and drink at the same time."

Niall snickered. "Ye're an arse."

"Aye, 'haps I am."

They were silent for a few minutes, Niall deep in thought as he stroked Prince's soft muzzle. His mind was a torment of unanswered questions. "Walter, I…I dinna know what to do."

"Take it one day at a time, brother. But do take it. No more being locked in your chamber."

Niall nodded even though his brother couldn't see him. A phantom twinge of pain rippled through the arm that was no longer there, and he stopped himself from moving to rub the spot, not wanting to humiliate himself in front of his brother. When would those pains go away? When would his body realize his arm had long since become bone in the earth?

One day at a time. That was something he might be able to do. "I'll have bad days."

"Aye. And good ones, too."

Niall nodded. He longed to saddle Prince and go for a ride but realized he wasn't even certain how to mount with only one arm to grab hold of the saddle. "I have so much to learn."

"Aye. But as I recall, ye're a fast learner."

"I'll start training again tomorrow."

"Good."

"But I willna be laird. Walter, the right to rule is yours now."

"Ye've time before ye need to make that choice. Da is yet breathing and making a ruckus."

"Aye. But I want ye to know what's coming. No matter what, I canna do that. I have to learn to pull on my bloody shirt first."

Walter slapped him on the back and squeezed his shoulder. "The lairdship is yours, with or without a shirt. Only thing I want is my brother back."

Niall drew in a long, mournful breath. "I'm not sure he's coming back. Ye'll have to learn to deal with me, the new me."

"New ye, old ye, still *ye*."

Want to read the rest of The Highlander's Gift?

Made in the USA
Columbia, SC
24 November 2023

27052992R00136